DEATH
IN A
SMALL TOWN

DEATH
IN A
SMALL TOWN

John Hedges

AIDAN ELLIS

First published in the United Kingdom by
Aidan Ellis Publishing, Cobb House, Nuffield,
Henley-on-Thames, Oxon RG9 5RT

First edition 1995

Copyright © John Hedges
The right of John Hedges to be identified as author of this
work has been asserted by him in accordance with the
Copyright Designs and Patents Act 1988

All rights reserved
Without limiting the rights under copyright reserved above, no
part of this publication may be reproduced, stored in or
introduced into a retrieval system or transmitted in any form
or by any means (electronic, mechanical, photocopying,
recording or otherwise) without the prior written permission of
both the copyright owner and the above publisher of this book

A CIP catalogue record for this book is
available from the British Library

Filmset in Plantin by
Contour Typesetters, Southall, Middx UB2 4BD
Printed in Britain by Biddles Ltd, Guildford, GU1 1DA

ISBN 0 85628 268 5

You are there from the stumbling beginnings of an unravelling story of twists and turns, mystery and excitement. It is so real in the telling – the less than lovely inside view of a premier archaeological discovery, the private magic wrung through long knowing from the dull setting of Ramsgate – so apparently real that it must be stated that **Death in a Small Town** *is* fiction.

But in his first novel John Hedges uses the simulation of fact as a device, not so much to spin a gripping tale with, as to depart from anything so obvious. The protagonist and his *alter ego*, first made significant to you by the events they are caught up in, show – as the focus shifts – how hollow a definition such is for any of us. And with truth, in any case, proving elusive and fickle; with the key points of who a person is (who we are) strangely impermanent; with even time itself becoming a little shaky – a situation is progressively brought about where both narrator *and* reader have to think . . .

This is a book of satisfying complexity – at different levels existentialist, an event-based thriller, *and* part of the coming 'men are human too' genre. It is also thoroughly and compulsively enjoyable.

To Erica and Jane

PART ONE

I

I now have only vague impressions of the day on which this story can be said to have begun. It wasn't so long ago but, I suppose, a lot has occurred since – and there were the circumstances.

My mother had died and I had driven to my home town. Her death was not unexpected but, for all that, the news was sudden and I drove as one shaken awake and as yet unbreakfasted. The route was something I could cope with mechanically, dimly aware of the all-too-familiar landmarks of each stage.

My thoughts were a different matter and I failed to focus them except, with effort, on being glad (really) for her sake and being concerned for my father. Actually, I do remember an obsession with the absence of a lavatory for almost the whole distance from Cambridge. I also remember coming to at the sight of the outskirts of Ramsgate and my heart sinking – but only as it always did.

When I arrived – in a metaphorical cloud of dust – I found that my father had already pulled himself together and my mother's body had gone, been taken. All that remained to be done was to wait for the funeral; a few days in limbo, a stagnant no-man's-land of time.

'Stagnant no-man's-land of time', what a fine phrase, but whoever reads this will have to make allowances, for I'm not at my best. In a way I never have been at my best – oh dear, that doesn't make sense. Stop! What do I mean? I'm so dosed I find it difficult to think. What I am trying to say is that I'm not feeling at all well and, in any case, I don't have facilities beyond what's needed to write a letter! So, I'm afraid, it has to be as it comes.

I suppose I was also starting to touch upon a subject which I'm finding difficult though, heaven knows, I can't avoid alluding to myself and my general situation, when I was so involved – when it wouldn't have happened without me. But . . . I can't explain – it's enough to say that I'm going to stick to what's necessary for the sake of the story.

Dear me, I am doing poorly, and I know it. The story, that's the issue. Aspects of it are well known, headline stuff – but there's the point. The whole truth is something which I've kept to myself till now and I somehow feel obligated to set the record straight.

I've just gone over what I wrote – and I got it wrong. It wasn't the day my mother died but a day or two after, when I was with my father: it was then that the seemingly trivial event occurred which was really the beginning. Other than that, I don't suppose I started off too badly, though I slid rapidly downhill – hardly surprising considering the condition I was in. Not that I feel *that* much better today, but I am more human – and certainly not as muddled. Mind, with the correction I've mentioned, what's written will have to do – no time for redrafts – to have begun at all is the thing.

But I think on reflection that this, if you like, false start has, in its way, been fortunate. On first re-reading I had wondered how I could be so obscure about what I was on about. If I'd felt even, say, as I feel today I would, without thought, have announced the conclusion from the outset – and I would have gone on to relate how that conclusion was reached from the point of view of hindsight. There would be nothing wrong with doing it that way – but that wasn't how it happened. I didn't know at any one point how things were going to evolve – far from it! This is itself an important element of the story, as is the manner in which matters were gradually brought to light.

I am rationalizing here, making what I'm going to do fit with, how did I put it, 'feeling obligated to perform some sort of duty'. I'll be saying next that the approach I am taking will make it more interesting to read. Well, maybe it will, but it's fast dawning on me that a large measure of what this is really about is that I want to relive the experience for myself through the mind-concentrating act of writing it down. I wonder why.

If I'm truthful I also have to say that in my present state it's going to be easier for me to simply start at the beginning . . . I haven't the head for anything smarter . . . and the telling will jog my memory.

So, after that diversion, I'll go back to a day or two after my mother had died, to me trailing up a road, after my surviving aged parent. He and I had, as per usual, walked to town by the cliff-capping promenade, trophy of retirement and otherwise now much used by dogs. I do remember that on the way down I had got him to stop and look momentarily at the large deserted house that had always held a great fascination for me but - even given the situation - I expect growth of the normal antagonistic separateness was well advanced. Certainly, the bloom had gone entirely by the time we were executing the daily pattern of unembellished manoeuvres in the town from the small brown loaf shop (where my father touched his hat to the assistant) to the paper shop, via a selection of such plain fare as a pound of Cox's apples, a pig's knee, and some Brussels sprouts. Then he was off home like a pigeon; there was never enough to fill the two string bags he always took and which he was carrying briskly on ahead. His very walk was expressive - at one and the same time - of both how sprightly and able he was (for his years), and the relationship between him and me, pacing behind, eyes to the ground, nothing in hand.

I'm afraid it is just one of those things that I have always walked with my head down, looking. Fellow archaeologists do not seem to do it - so that is one theory spoiled - and are as nonplussed as others at my pouncing excitement over small change or my stopping and puzzling over something which may be worthless, ordinary, and broken.

We had just reached the hospital, a rather nondescript, single-storey, between-the-wars pocket labyrinth with cars arranged on next to no frontage and what would pass for an inner-city hedge. I remember the bus-stop with the polygonally-sectioned post of sandy, lichen-covered concrete, the pavement with only slightly textured cement flagstones, the pinker, arched shelter with the seat inside, the graffiti and litter. I remember the kerbed start of the bed of the hedge and noticing how the green was towards the top, with the bottom half all bare lank stems, and how underneath were dry brown privet leaves, and more litter. It was among those leaves that I saw a glint of green; I stopped and knelt down. What I found was not just one coin, its surface bright with copper oxide, but a group of five. It was curious - and I immediately saw it as such - but, particularly in the circumstances, it was (as I have said) a seemingly trivial occurrence. I feel I have represented it faithfully. My father had not even stopped; I put the coins in my pocket and walked, for a while, with a quickened pace.

While the kettle was being put on, I went out to the garage to look for the brass-bristled suede brush I knew was somewhere there. In the short time it had taken me to put the five green discs into my pocket, I had instinctively realized that not only were they not current coin of the realm but also that they never had been. Such would have been equally obvious to anyone who has collected from childhood. But what was puzzling me continued to do so as I brushed the loose, bright oxide from first one coin and then another. They were of copper; they were of the same denomination and type; and beneath the very superficial and recent corrosion, they were in uniformly mint condition. The problem was that I couldn't identify them and I went back into the house – running the gauntlet of lunch being in preparation – to get the magnifying glass from the drawer where it was always kept. What was on the coins was as clear as day, but incomprehensible. On the one side was 'East India Company' around an armorial device with the date, 1808, below it: the design on the other side was even more mysterious, consisting mostly of Arabic lettering, except at the bottom where there was 'X CASH'.

Later, I went down to the reference room of the public library for the first time since I too – albeit rarely – had sat there in my uniform after school. The slightly grander than small-townness of it swept me with a sense of claustrophobia and of anguish; it was as though the good fathers of the municipality had bounded aspiration in image of their own. It was a very poignant feeling and, without a mission, I would have left. As it was, I was able to leaf through a 'catalogue of world coins' and, with surprisingly little trouble, to identify my finds. Actually, I found out nothing more than I already knew, but it somehow satisfies collectors to see things listed.

I chuckled over this as I started back for my father's house; it made me think of something, by coincidence to do with coins, which I had been completely taken up with in Cambridge before having been called away, and which had slipped my mind.

But then my thoughts shifted again and I felt glad that I had walked – it was the slow and close level at which I had experienced that town. Coins, however, seemed to be the order of the day and I stopped briefly outside a house where seeming centuries ago a friend and I had haggled with another boy (I presume known to him) and had come away with five coins for nine old pence each. I remembered how there were five and how suspicious but daring we had been, for they were a mystery to us: one was a forgery – at least it melted; two were bought by the dealer we then rushed to (I would guess now that they were Indo-Greek – they were obscure); my friend was left with what turned out to be a silver drachm of the Parthian emperor Mithradates II;

while I had (and still have) what I eventually discovered to be a coin of the immediately pre-Roman period in Spain.

Then again, and among many anecdotes that could have come to mind from the far past, there was the wooden 'mace' – a sort of parade leader's staff (we thought it Masonic) – which appeared from somewhere. It was dark brown and varnished, with a knob at one end and a rather thick, but tapered, hexagonal shaft – a bit like a table leg; what was odd was that each of its sides had Roman coins pinned to it by tight circles of little brass nails. The thing was of course stripped by us and then discarded – even its head sawn in two, to be sure – and heaven knows what happened to all the coins, though I do have a few still, dark-glossy on one side.

I suppose I was absentmindedly giving some place, a relevance, to my little find of the day. But it went a bit further than that, for it brought to mind that the Cambridge project I spoke of was the first time my hobby started in childhood had actually played any part in my now professional work – perhaps surprisingly so. Anyway, the memories flooded in, in quite an unusually warm and pleasant way and – in spite of the circumstances – I went to sleep that night feeling strangely satisfied, enthusiastic and excited. I had put the five ten-cash pieces of the East India Company on the chest of drawers next to my bed and gave them a last look before switching off the light.

II

I don't know what happened with the next day. Well, I do really. On the one hand, we went to get a death certificate and to deliver it to the undertaker; on the other hand, my awareness matured of just how unbearably stifling, restraining, and agitating I found visiting Ramsgate, indeed visiting home. I put this irrelevant divergence here for a purpose and that is as an act of self-discipline, the deliberate drawing of a line. I do feel that introducing what I have to say via some reference to my family circumstances and my family relations was the easiest way. But, even if this subject were interesting, it is not relevant, and I feel I should shutter it out as far as I can. This, I can see, is likely to lead to a certain amount of artificiality; but so be it – I'll do my best to round the corners. But, on reflection, the idea of being a detached agent, that little bit of 'artistic licence', does actually overlap with the truth.

The point is that the day following – the Thursday, the day before the funeral – I woke with a quiet determination that I was going to do something that I wanted to do, on my own, and that I wasn't going to be thwarted. One has these feelings of being paralysed but still conscious of wanting, wanting, to break out – there are many analogies – and I had learnt that the only salvation – if one could find, embrace, and doggedly pursue it – was an objective, no matter how small. And I had an objective. Being woken with a mug of stewed tea pregnant with lateness had no effect – I had already worked out for what proportion of a century it was that I had exclusively drunk coffee at that time of day, and I was through the tired phase of wondering why I couldn't stay in bed when, for once in a hectic life, there was nothing to hurry about. I left the tea and was equally impervious to the 'I've had my breakfast, what do you want?' routine (accompanied by hovering in outdoor shoes and jacket with one eye on the washing up, yet to be generated, that would need to be done before going out). I don't know what happens to all the small brown loaves in Christendom come nine o'clock and I do appreciate that one has 'to get something for lunch' (daily?) but I just said:

'I've got somewhere to go today, I'll wash up, and I won't be back for lunch.'

Of course, it wasn't actually that simple but I'll leave things with the clean-cut image of him going off in a huff with his bicycle clips; and me going where I wanted to go slightly later. No, it wasn't as simple as that, but it was the turning point connected with this story that made me say there was actually some truth in the idea of my having become detached. Two days earlier I had declared why I was going to the public library – and had reported my findings – but from that Thursday on I kept things to myself. With hindsight, I can now see that having a purpose and a private world echoed how I'd broken out and had a free existence in my youth; somehow, in the conciliatory well-past-adolescence days I had become enmeshed again.

I am getting ahead of myself here. My objective that particular day saw no further than itself and, now I come to think of it, was an embarrassingly trivial one – a token of the degree of my plight. Since finding the five coins, I had noticed (or re-noticed) a junk shop – itself not far from the hospital. In the window, along with a lot of other miscellaneous 'tutt', I had seen in passing that there were some open boxes of rubbishy coins at so much each, as well as several individually priced, in packets. There was nothing I had seen that I would have wanted to bother about in the normal course of events. But, as I have indicated, finding that odd little cache had triggered a lot of memories in me. All I wanted to do was to go down to the shop – on foot and via some alleyways – and have a look through the coins.

Before I actually went in I stood and savoured the moment. The sort of shop I am talking about is not really a junk shop, in the sense of stocking secondhand trash but, equally, one would overdignify it and its wares by the use of the word 'antique'. I know what I mean. Such shops brim full of fascinating bits and pieces from a past which is just out of reach; objects which can be measured to one's purse, which can be possessed and collected; small treasures that one can only recognize for oneself, and which themselves fire enthusiasm and light fresh avenues. My eye was caught by postcards, medals, stamps, cap badges and militaria. I wondered who bought the ornaments of china, brass, and what-have-you – and I thought, not for the first time, what a very curious phenomenon 'ornaments' are. I have to say that I experienced shock at seeing that things current when I was young were now, for some, 'pieces from the past which is just out of reach'. But while thus taking in and musing on the whole, my attention quickly settled on the coins. I did not allow myself to register any more than that they were there before pushing open the shop door in full anticipation that this would cause a bell to be struck. Which it did.

'Hello. I'd like to have a look at the coins in the window, please.' For some reason, the 'properness' of my diction jarred on me.

'Any in particular?' the man asked, getting up, folding his paper.

'No, no,' I responded, 'them all.'

As he shuffled crablike among the clutter behind the counter I had a feeling I knew him; there was something in the mannerisms of this wiry, smoked man, now clearly beyond 'retirement age', that made him seem familiar. Ah, yes, I was in George Street but he used to have a similar shop on King Street – we actually called him 'King Street'. I had to smile (to myself) when he gave me just one of the boxes, reserving the rest on his side of the counter. At least he went back to his paper without a word. I went slowly through the boxes, and then through the packets. Other people came and went; nothing of moment happened. In the end I had a little pile of stuff – or more exactly, I self-consciously had a number of little piles equating to the number of boxes, together with some packets. And what a load of old rubbish what I had amounted to. I cannot remember them all now but there was a bronze coin of Napoleon III, about the size of an old penny; a halfpenny piece of George III (which you could only just make out as such); a much damaged 'cartwheel' penny; a William IV groat, rubbed flat and plugged; an Edward VII florin; several farthings (including blackened ones); a silver three-pence; and a 1953 type set in a sealed plastic wallet. In pride of place was a rather worn and knocked Victorian crown (old head) and a George II shilling, perforated but with 'LIMA' below the bust. There was more – it came to over twenty pounds' worth of sheer folly and must have made his day; not that he was in any way communicative until he had the money.

I asked to look around and, while he had left me in peace before, he now struck up a desultory conversation. This was partly my due as a proven customer but was also, I felt, in hopes of massaging further sales; he hadn't quite made me out. I browsed, but one thing I saw and picked up almost imperceptibly threw him off balance, for just a split second. He took a cigarette from an open packet on the counter, lit it, and casually asked if I knew what it was I was holding. I did know, and from habit I took the opportunity of establishing my credentials on something I didn't want.

'It's a chain-mail piercing dagger. Indian. You hold it in a clenched fist, like this.'

I was slightly disconcerted by his expressionless response and bemused by what he said.

'Well, if you're interested in that sort of thing you've missed your chance. There was a bit of it about, I understand.' He gave me a knowing look and produced a heavily doodled-on Xerox of a typewritten sheet; it was a police list and, for my benefit, he underlined 'Antiques of Indian description'. 'That,' he said, nodding towards the weapon still in my hand, 'I've had that a long time; may have come with the shop! It's a good price if you want it; no call round here,' he added.

I suddenly understood and let him know in an inconsequential way that I'd merely thought the dagger of passing interest; that I was visiting the town, for a few days, but had lived there; and that I collected generally. This worked, and I went on to say, 'You used to have a shop in King Street, didn't you?'

With that the conversation warmed up quite a bit and from time to time, *a propos* of nothing, he pulled illicit tit-bits from his desk drawers – just like he used to. It was entirely typical that – having made a great show all the while of secretively closing the drawers – he should leave the top one open just sufficiently for me to be able to see a small packet of coins of quite characteristic type in it.

'What about the Roman coins?' I asked, predictably.

'Oh,' he said 'I've promised those to someone. They're put by. Sorry!'

I looked disappointed.

'Hang on a minute,' he continued, conspiratorially, and then he did something which I would have paid money to have seen. He pretended to look up a number; dialled (possibly his own home); and had an imaginative one-sided conversation. I was spellbound.

'He says he's coming in for them this afternoon but I said I couldn't guarantee to hold them,' he told me (rather unnecessarily), opened the drawer, got out a piece of green baize, and tipped the contents of the packet on to it. 'Fifty quid the lot. Cash. Can't split them. Other chap sells on to the trade in London. They're good, but you'll know that.'

It was an Oscar-winning performance, and I was appreciative of his art. The coins? Well, they would have impressed the uninitiated and he'd evidently summed me up on the basis of what I'd already bought. It was a small handful of third-century 'radiates' and undistinguished fourth-century bronzes, all legible, but not in the best of condition. 'Radiates', oh yes – named after the spiked crown the emperor was depicted wearing. Anyway, I took my time, holding each one to the light and turning it over; this was partly because I didn't know what to do, but partly because it is only by looking hard that one is going to recognize something obscure. It was while I was examining the coins that the arrival of some boys outside was heralded by voices and a clatter of bicycles. But just as one got to the door, the others looking over his shoulder, they were waved away with sudden firmness by the shopkeeper.

'They're a bloody nuisance that lot,' he explained. 'Always in here.'

The Roman coins were not of any interest in their own right but I was idly struck by two things. First, their patina and its condition suggested the coins had been found recently and, in all likelihood, in the neighbourhood. Second, according to one of my 'principles', there was the question of what was missing – for the coins I saw were obviously just a selection from what would actually have been found. I asked, but I could read that he didn't have anything else and that I wasn't going to shift him from the wicket he was playing of such as he was showing me being 'hard to come by'. Still, I had made my interests plain, there were prospects, and I said with sincerity that, having come across him again after so many years, I'd look in whenever I was in Ramsgate to see what he'd got. This was a bit tongue in cheek for it was clear that, for all his smiles, generalized reminiscences and affirmations, he had no recollection of me whatsoever.

III

I had only just got out of the shop, and slightly past it, when I was ambushed by the boys who had been turned away. They swooped from the higher ground and pulled up next to me.

'We saw you looking at the Roman coins' and 'You a dealer?' two of them said – I wasn't sure which, or in what order.

I, meanwhile, was getting in the way of people on the narrow path and generally drifting downhill; the boys were in various stages of being on their bikes and off them, jockeying for position, and causing equivalent obstruction in the road.

'Look,' I said, pointing a short distance, 'go on ahead to where the bench is.'

They went without a word and stood in a group where the pavement extended back. There were four of them, all wearing the anonymous jeans and jumpers of youth. I'm not at all good at ages but it occurred to me that three were, maybe, thirteen or fourteen, and the other a bit younger. Of the older three: one had a parting; another black hair, combed straight back; and the third wore glasses.

'So,' I remarked, 'what can I do for you?' There was an air of trepidation, tinged with vying excitement.

The earlier questions were repeated by the two at the front, the one with the parting (James) saying they had seen me with the Roman coins, and the one with swept-back hair (Brian) interjecting to ask me again if I was a 'dealer'. The smallest (Paul) burst in with the statement that 'they had taken them there', an utterance quickly covered by the bespectacled Peter, who wanted to know if I'd 'bought any'. It was like a ragged peal of bells. I put the names here because they were soon enough known to me: Paul and Peter, incidentally, were brothers.

I told them that the coins were interesting so far as they went but that they weren't all there. What omniscience! And I left my status enigmatic.

'But the man in the shop said we should only leave the clearest ones with him,' James volunteered.

'So as he could check them in a book he keeps at home to value them and offer them as a "lot" to a dealer,' said Brian.

I was rather expecting young Paul to say something next but he appeared to have been silenced. His brother glanced across at James and muttered, 'And the ones we didn't take.'

I asked Brian directly, intrigued, how much they thought they were going to get. 'Well,' he answered in a very man-of-the-world way, 'he reckoned if he sold them as a "lot" to a London dealer who specialized we'd probably get fifteen.' He thought himself remarkably clever for having inflated the figure.

'Do you want to see the other stuff?' asked James. 'We can always get the ones in the shop back.'

'For fifteen,' came in Brian.

'We split them up, apart from one or two we haven't decided on,' Peter said. 'We only live up St Lawrence.'

'I'll tell you what,' I said, clinching matters, 'I could meet you outside St Lawrence in maybe half an hour's time.'

Watches were synchronized (I never wear one) and they hightailed off with as much talking between them as was practicable. I walked on as soon as they were out of sight, fairly briskly, and along a route which I had hastily put together in my mind. The whole business of the man in the shop and of the boys had amused me no end and I was still mulling it over, betweentimes, when I saw that Brian (alone) had got to the church before me. I felt that this was a pity since I'd planned to cast an idle eye over the outside of the building, now questioning my uncritical acceptance of it as 'Norman', full stop. Anyway, Brian was there, with his split of the additional coins, and what he basically wanted was to come to some sort of deal whereby he would sell his share to me and then act as an intermediary if I wanted the remainder. He was still in the early stages of arguing this proposition when the others arrived – themselves cautiously before time. What their friend may have been up to clearly didn't occasion much surprise, or merit any response beyond ostensible disregard.

The coins, fourth part and total, had among them exactly what I wanted, and the little thrill that went through me brought a focus to my mind and interest. Why I wanted these small, irregular, green, virtually featureless little discs I will be explaining later, as I will the general difficulty of obtaining them. Sufficient to say now that they were there in front of my eyes – a good fifty, plus other odds and ends – and that I managed to strike a bargain. The boys had mixed feelings, I could see. Partly this was because their shares, products of many a minor battle, were simply amalgamated, and partly because it is one thing to feel that you have something of value, and another thing to part with it. I actually gave them about twice the going rate, though as young Paul (correctly) divulged, 'It won't even pay for the batteries.' But, as I said, feelings while mixed were, on balance, happy enough.

Though the business was done I still wanted to fish for information and, if possible, to keep up the contact. 'You lot come across many coins?' I asked.

'Oh, yeah,' said Brian casually.

According to Paul they came by 'modern' and 'loads of pre-decimal, some silver'; he added that they sometimes got 'foreign' from the arcades. Peter said they bought 'English' from dealers.

Brian clearly didn't think this impressive. 'Well,' he said, 'there's been other things you know.' (Man-of-the-world pause.) 'Gotta keepa turnover.' (Pause.) 'Some as hot as curry.' (Smile.) 'Got it from a jumble sale.' (Smile.) 'Had to ditch it. Sold one or two pieces of gold too.' (Shrug of the shoulders.) 'What you interested in?' (Head jerked up a fraction and then to one side.)

I could just imagine him selling his grandfather's sovereigns for ready cash; I focused things in reaction. 'I'm rather keen on the Roman coins you had,' I said. 'I might well want some more,' I continued, gritting my teeth, 'if they were all from a site round here.' It was put neatly.

Peter and James were still in an exchange of eye contact which had started while I had been talking to Brian. I mistakenly took this for reluctance to tell me anything about the site – though they were certainly all evasive on that issue.

'It's a place out past Sarre where we've got permission,' volunteered Brian. 'Farmer said not to tell anyone else.'

I couldn't resist pointing out that 'out past Sarre' would have been water in Roman times.

'Well, thereabouts,' Brian rejoindered. 'Can't expect us to tell you exactly.'

'Is it Richborough?' I asked pointedly.

There was a shaking of heads.

'It's definitely not Richborough?' I said. 'Richborough is legally protected – terrible trouble.'

'It is definitely not Richborough,' answered James.

I had got somewhere, though I wasn't going to get any further, and my conscience had benefitted from the line of thought that things could have been worse. All I wanted to do now was to be congenial.

'Have you all got metal-detectors?' I asked.

I expected to be deluged with names of models and with technicalities which I would nod at in an interested fashion, asking the odd intelligent question. The fact was that all they had between them was a sort of junior model, which Paul had had for Christmas and which was hijacked by his elder brother (for a share) after James had discovered an archaeological site and managed to enthuse his two contemporaries. Brian, it seems, had assumed the role of 'business manager'.

I couldn't help but enquire how the site had been found but, before James could come back to me, young Paul had jumped in . . .

'You can see things – pits and things – near the top of the cliff, from the beach.'

The mention of cliffs brought the location very much closer to home and both James and Brian were visibly annoyed with Paul, and rounded on him over a chasm of age difference.

'Why don't you go home now?' snapped one.

'Yeah, we'll give Peter your share for you. Beat it!' said the other.

Paul was quick to retort. 'You won't get my metal-detector again, will they, Peter?'

'And,' said Peter, 'what about the coins you haven't come up with yet, James?'

James was angry, fed up, and caught out. He shoved his hand into his jeans' pocket and pulled out three largish first/second-century bronze coins.

'You got more of the other ones,' he remonstrated, 'I wanted to keep these, remember? We agreed!'

'But the others got all mixed back together, didn't they?' asked Peter.

'That's right,' declared Brian, just realizing.

James was reddening and defensive. 'If you feel like that, just split the money between you.'

'But we don't know whether those coins aren't worth a fortune,' pursued Peter. 'We might be getting diddled.'

I felt I should intervene. Partly because I had an interest, and partly to put matters right; I'd also, however – even on such short acquaintance – developed something of a soft spot for James and I thought he was being hard done by. I studied the coins in question in a slow, deliberate and authoritative way. James meanwhile was telling me that each was of the early empire, the largest one 'of Claudius', and how he had found the site, and how this fitted in with the invasion of Britain, and how he was now finding bits of pottery and other objects in the field. It was all quite low-scale and naive – and the coin of Claudius, worn smooth, was more probably of Galba – but he was very involved and his horizons went beyond the obvious and the immediately to hand.

'In this sort of shape,' I said, 'coins like these have little or no commercial value.'

'That's just what I told you, isn't it?' cut in Brian.

'Well, that's right,' I agreed, 'but James obviously has an interest in them in relation to the site. As Peter says, though, there ought to be a small financial adjustment.'

It was soon settled and everyone was happy. They were vastly impressed when I handed my card round with the injunction that they should keep in touch. James read the card closely and looked up at me, 'You're an archaeologist are you? I mean, a real one?'

IV

The fact that I was an archaeologist was giving me a problem of conscience and I must explain this, as I must also explain the interest in these small, irregular, green, virtually featureless little discs which I have mentioned.

At the time of which I am writing, archaeology as a profession was in a state of self-conscious metamorphosis, complete with growing pains. The territory was being staked out and legally claimed by a new strain while the old ways were being marginalized and made to look low. Oh, it is unassailably correct that the importance of a non-renewable resource should be recognized and that it should be the curatorial preserve of the properly qualified and appointed. Clear, too, that such remains – small and large, seen and unseen, understood and not understood, exciting and dreary – should not be investigated (unless unavoidable) but should be protected and left undisturbed for posterity. Obvious, too, that the whole business could only be effectively regulated and monitored by mechanisms of local and national government. I agree. At the same time, it was passing difficult to reconcile this drift with the excitement that the very mention of the word 'archaeology' kindled in me. The subject was becoming a bit grey. And if the happy amateur and the academic in unhampered pursuit of a thread of knowledge with spade and trowel were now as much of our past as the grave-robber and landed dilettante, imagine the anathema with which the metal-detector operator was regarded.

'Metal-detectors' – for those who have never heard of them – are a civilian refinement of the land-mine detectors of the Second World War; shaped and used like an upright vacuum cleaner, they transmit an altered note to headphones when there is metal below the ground surface. In their new incarnation they have become more sensitive, and some can even discriminate between different metals. There was a craze – possibly still is – when people (mainly boys and men) moved up and down wet fields and deserted strands in detached slow motion, sweeping their machines from side to side before them. Occasionally they were rewarded with Civil War hoards, Iron Age torcs, or mediaeval chalices, but finds were more usually a back-breaking succession of ring-pulls, nails, small change, and other fractions of the unbelievable density of metallic detritus which is everywhere. Though hope and enthusiasm may no doubt feed each other, the average rate of return for hours put in is laughable and the pursuit has all the charm, to the unattracted, of sitting next to a grimy canal in the rain catching nothing worth having.

Metal-detecting provoked a knee-jerk reaction from the archaeological lobby, which rallied to the flag and denounced enthusiasts as looters who should be viewed as pariahs. It is true that an object could be ripped from its context, and there were dreadful cases of archaeological sites being targetted and vandalized. At the same time, most finds were actually from ploughsoil (the machines had limited range) and they had got there largely as a result of the destruction of archaeological sites by post-war methods of intensive farming; the archaeologists were bravely chasing the hyenas from the carcase. Metal-detecting was a phenomenon thrown into relief by the accident of occurring at a transitional stage; there was no right or wrong in a black and white sense, it was just a matter of a subject entering its second estate and tilting its nose at the living embodiment of its own origins. Whatever the benefits, I cannot help but feel a pang for that generation of youthful new enthusiasts who found that a line had been drawn, and that they were on the wrong side of it.

So there you have the reason why I, a middle-aged, respectable archaeologist living and working in Cambridge, was having a crisis of conscience over an enabling relationship with a group of metal-detecting kids from where I came from. Of course, if generations could be contemporaries, I had a foot in each camp, for there is no doubt that if I had been a child at that time I would have been filled with the craze. But even in the unsophisticated time framework of the then and there, there was ambivalence in my mind and that, if you like, was the deeper source of my unease.

What I was doing on a day-to-day basis by way of work then was bringing together all the various elements of reports on archaeological excavations that had taken place (in advance of development) on extensive ploughed-out sites. All that was left was filled-in ditches, post-holes, and foundation trenches, everything that didn't penetrate the gravel just having been churned into the topsoil. Most of the sites had a large element of Roman archaeology to them and one of the main categories of objects was coins. These were identified, analysed, and written up by a specialist at a museum – but they had an interest for me and, in a way, also revived an interest. What caught my attention, in my own peculiar way, was not the coins that could be readily matched with known and catalogued types but the item upon item in the listings simply dismissed as '3rd (or 4th) century barbarous'.

I did not really have any quarrel with the idea that, in parts of the third and of the fourth centuries AD, crisis inflation and/or political disruption caused the official base-metal coinage to be supplemented by local products. Such low-value small change was aptly described as 'barbarous' in that – to a greater or smaller degree – design and lettering went native while size was often skimped. But I felt there was a trap here, for the category was just a residual slot; the less intelligible something was the more likely it was to belong. I had the suspicion that the one explanation was not sufficient for all the little green discs that turned up – particularly the nastier ones.

And my suspicion had a root and took me in a direction. As everyone knows, Roman Britain became Saxon England when the Western Empire collapsed under barbarian pressure in the early 400s. But it really couldn't have been that simple; one thing is that the province would have been coming apart and becoming detached for a while; the other is that Romano-British culture would not have vanished overnight, for by then it was indigenous and was all that people had known for centuries. My query was over the coinage – I couldn't help but wonder if some of the barbarous issues, rather than being contemporary with the official ones they imitated, were not stylistic copies in continuation of a fading tradition. If sub-Roman local leaders had sprung up in the political vacuum – even for a short time – what, after all, would their coinage have looked like? And, in any case, I was greatly encouraged in this thought by the fact that several of the minute silver sceattas of the Early Saxons had designs which, though degraded, clearly came from Roman originals. It had been assumed that there hadn't been a copper coinage, but was that assumption correct?

By hunch or reason I turned not to the barbarous versions of the fourth-century coins but to the imitations of those of the third – the so-called 'radiates'. This was strange logic, looking back a century and a half, but I had a feeling about it. From a British viewpoint of the time, the majority of copper coins with the emperor wearing a distinctive spiked radiate crown had not been issued by the central authority but by two long-lasting and successful rebellions which attempted to throw off that authority. The one was the so-called 'Gallic Empire' (Gaul, Britain and Spain), founded by Postumus, in the third quarter of the third century; the other, the holding out of Britain under Carausius and then Allectus at the end of the third century. Coins of this period are found commonly to this day, and what I felt was that the 'radiate' may have become identified in the declining years of the Roman Empire with rebellion and self-determination.

So I began spending evenings on a slightly secretive project in which I went through all of the barbarous radiates from all of the sites, looking, looking, looking, looking. By and large I got nowhere – some of the coins were simply local (contemporary) copies, good or bad; others were too corroded for one to be sure about anything; while only a few were sufficiently odd to give any continued encouragement. Definition of this oddness was elusive and I entered into a programme of compiling a cumulative catalogue of record cards with scaled photographic enlargements. I had the unhappy feeling that the project as a whole was going the way of most academic research – from original and bright conception, through a quickening mire of data gathering, to uncertainty and hedged-about conclusions. And then it happened!

It was one of those moments of heart-stopping ecstatic excitement that can never be forgotten. The coin I had put on the stage of the binocular low-powered microscope (it was the only way) was particularly clear. The head was a bit schematized, but only a bit; the beard, face, and radiate crown held together as a portrait of sorts. The letters were well defined but, as is not uncommon, made little sense in terms of any known emperor's legend. I could so easily have just written down 'copy, good local style, with blundered, unintelligible legend', and would have, except that – to my astonishment – one of the letters was not of the Roman alphabet, but unique to the Anglo-Saxon. It looked like a lower case *d* with a bent crossed vertical – ᚧ – it was a *thorn*, the sound made through parted teeth blocked by the tongue, the one rendered in modern English as *th* – as in *th*e, *th*is, *th*us, and *th*erefore. The jumble of letters was a jumble no more for it spelt AELTHRED, a good enough Saxon name (even if, as it turned out, it was otherwise unrecorded) and obviously a minor king who had been lost to history.

Well, my euphoria can be imagined and was all the better for the private pleasure of the whole enterprise. And I went on immediately after that evening, in a frenzy of continued excitement, to check through published early documentary sources and to microphotograph the whole of the coin, just the portion of the legend, and the letter in question, differently lit, and printed to varying scales. It's a funny thing to say in contrast but the coin – to this day – remains unpublished, Aelthred is as unknown about as before its discovery, and – as far as I know – barbarous issues are still regarded in the way that they were. I think only someone with similar experiences could understand how this could be but, somehow – and it has happened to me more than once – a breakthrough just leads to a pressing desire to take things further, and the more complex and time-consuming something becomes, the more likely it is to evaporate, to be overtaken, or simply to be pushed to one side by practical considerations.

What took my attention away in this case will become manifestly obvious, but it is more than germane to point out what was in the front of my mind in the wake of the discovery of the Aelthred coin. What was needed was not the dribs and drabs of specimens that came my way from a limited number of archaeological sites – and which I had exhausted as a current resource – but hundreds and thousands of prospective examples that could be combed through. The proven potential of the exercise required no less and this, after all, is the way in which all comprehensive catalogues of coin types studied have been compiled. But the problem was that museums – coming from the art historical side – had not been disposed to purchase and hoard masses of horrid little coins over the decades against the possibility that someone in the future might discover that they were really very interesting and worth having. No, the way to get enough of these little coins to study, which – apart from other considerations, would be difficult to spot with the naked eye – was by metal-detecting.

I chased the arguments round in my head until I had fixed them in a configuration that left me feeling justified about the course of action I was pursuing. I realize that I am not on firm ground now since the project didn't get anywhere, but I can point out that during this period pre-Roman coins came to be the more completely understood by exactly the same means.

V

It was just as well that I was happy about things for I had evidently spurred on the activities of what I dubbed 'the Ramsgate cell'. There in my pigeonhole on a bleary-eyed Monday morning three weeks later, among the sediment of book brochures and intimations from learned societies, was a letter in a childish hand on the sort of feint-lined 'azure' paper that comes in pads. No doubt there had been an envelope to match and I cringed at the thought of the letter having been opened by the secretary. One did get similar looking letters – mainly enquiries about 'digs' – and perhaps she'd been too preoccupied or idle to look at this one closely; on the other hand, inquisitiveness was another of her attributes; but then, the point at issue may have been lost on her, and besides, she was fairly well disposed towards me. Oh dear, I hadn't been very clever.

It was a letter from Brian and the main gist of it was that they had found 'two hundred and fifty-two' more coins (including 'many of the ones I was interested in'), that he'd got back those left with the shop-owner, and that he'd send the lot on receipt of a certain amount in postal orders. 'On receipt' was not the only fine and incongruous phrase among the poor grammar and spelling; there was also 'by return', 'postage and packing included' and, of course, 'Yours Faithfully'.

I always came away from Ramsgate and its personal connections with great relief and could not wait to reimmerse myself in the world that I had created elsewhere. At home there was the good tea and coffee, exotic foods, semi-antique furnishings, books, records and other stimuli; at work there was the academic and intellectual environment, a pleasant and worthwhile pursuit, rather than a brute trade of time for money. Most of all, it was simply the getting away from an oppressive, stifling and pricking situation I could not cope with, and the thought of going back with any immediacy was definitely never at the front of my mind. But, as the days passed, what

I had returned to became normal and, as time went on, I began to feel that I really should go down and see my ageing parents (or parent); this feeling generally surfaced about the third week, meaning that I went every month (unless it had been especially bad on the previous occasion). The letter from Brian was, as it happened, very timely and I wrote back (from my home address) saying that I would buy the coins but wished to meet all four of them for this purpose on the following Saturday, at a particular time, near the bus-stop in Pegwell village.

I chose the location partly out of mischief since I knew the site must be near there; it was also my intention from the outset to go and have a look for myself after the meeting. While I waited I leaned over a wall which ran along the top of the cliff and looked down on a filled-in cove which had been a Victorian pleasure gardens, but which was now just waste ground. That whole area had once been considered a pleasurable charabanc destination from Ramsgate and I was musing on this when I became aware that the boys had arrived.

There were only three of them, young Paul was absent and his brother Peter looked decidedly uncomfortable, hovering on the edge of things. Come to that, James and Brian were ill at ease, something had clearly happened, and what this had been soon spilled out. Since my last visit the farmer had planted young cauliflowers and my confederates had been metal-detecting between the rows after dark, using torches where necessary. They had just been caught – I imagine an unnerving experience – and all hell had been let loose: there had been home visits by the local constabulary; their school had been informed; and the next edition of the local paper was an unwelcome prospect. As usual in such situations, all the half-truths told in conspiracy were naked and unglamorous in full light; parents, feeling both betrayed and guilty, were retrospectively zealous and too caring; and confederacy broke down into mutual recrimination 'our boy wouldn't have done that unless he'd been led on' coming to be believed, even by the malefactors as a convenient fiction. No wonder Paul was not there, and no wonder the other three looked so separate and eager to go. Did they blame me? – I realized with sudden horror my own implication in the affair; I felt red, embarrassed, caught out and saw that little bit more in the boys wanting to leave. Their reluctant half-answers only made it clearer that I had been invoked as a scapegoat *deus ex machina* but by some mercy they had not revealed my identity (lest I told the greater truth) and the police (whether they believed them or not) had let things go with a warning. Well, the show was over and I settled quickly for what had been brought – they wouldn't have come if they'd been empty-handed – and we then each went our own way, rather coolly.

I certainly felt subdued but was nevertheless determined to go and look for the site. As I turned along the start of the unmade cliff-top path I came upon James' bike and, looking over, saw him making his way down to the former pleasure grounds by way of a ledge cut into the cliff. He had just got to a vertical drop which I knew from when I was his age and, seeing me, he stopped and waved.

I closed the distance between us and said, pointing back along the cliff-top, 'I want to go to see the site.'

'So do I,' he replied, smiling, 'but, if it's all the same to you, we won't go that way.'

The difficulty of getting down that vertical drop was not the only change I saw among the sameness. Part of the sea wall of the pleasure grounds had collapsed – though I enjoyed pointing out lead bullets which the invading tide had left, evidence of reuse as a First World War pistol range. As I told James, as we walked along, I used to go thereabouts on my own every day some holidays. The wave-cut platform of chalk up to the cliff was the same, green-slimed, rock-pooled, and flint-strewn. And the caves were indistinguishable, even if I felt changes in their size and configuration. My attention, as always, was drawn to the fragile fossils enveloped within the mass of the chalk; those seen easily were already too broken and it took skill to spot the signs of one worth having – and then there was the (often wasted) patience required to dig it out before the tide came in. It was on looking up that one saw the change – though it had actually all been in my time; nothing much had happened since the power station (now in mothballs) had ruined the skyline and the 'hoverport' (empty and deserted) had wrecked the peace and obliterated an area of mudflats that everyone seemed to think vile. I don't like change and I think I felt it round there most of all; it certainly used to get to me when my father insisted on telling me the council's latest proposals for building a road up from the shore, over the whole lot.

We were walking and then I stopped and pointed upwards to where the chalk cliffs began to be replaced, from the top down, by the less stable red-brown, coarse silt known as 'Thanet Sands'.

James just looked at me and said, 'So you knew where it was, did you?'

I actually hadn't known, and I told him as much. What I had been pointing to was the geological formation, the edge of the solid rock of the Isle of Thanet cut away and then silted up against. It was in this broad band of silt that the Wantsum Channel, a mile wide in Roman times, had separated the island from the mainland, the fort of Richborough at its southern end, Reculvers at its northern. That was in Roman times, the Wantsum had all but silted up since, encouraged by early monkish land reclamation, while the infilling at the margins – such as we were looking at – was really very much older.

We made quite a joke of the fact that I hadn't spotted the site for myself. I'm not sure James absolutely believed me, but it was the truth and I found I was strangely pleased about it. What had thrown me, I think, *was* the geological configuration. I could now see in the cliff section how a settlement straddled the surface interface of the Thanet Sands and chalk. Features dug into the subsoil on the one hand jumbled up, contaminated and confused the Thanet Sands, while on the other hand they peppered and churned up the chalk to give a not dissimilar effect. But the worse the confusion the greater the activity, and it was there to be seen. James said that he'd only realized what it was when he came by immediately after part of the cliff top had collapsed in the last winter. Among the earth temporarily on the beach had been pottery fragments, pieces of bones and, most tellingly, a coin and part of a brooch. The brooch gave me sudden food for thought but I didn't interrupt, and he went on to relate how he'd had the idea of metal-detecting in the field above and how the others had become involved.

This last was said in a perceptibly regretful tone and I thought there had been more to it than their having been caught out. What I suspected was that the personally meaningful and magical had suffered, rather like something might begin to fade on contact with light or tarnish in the air. The other three may have been boys, and his friends, but in a relative way they were the world – the one with the bovine stare and thick-fingered brute evaluations. To Brian, after all, it could as well have been a matter of lead off church roofs (except, I understand, this substance had rather lost its value). And for Peter it was the kind of interest that schoolboys have and grow out of; one stage of several that sort of happen regardless of the degree of personal involvement. Paul was merely apeing those older. But to James, I guessed, the whole discovery had had much inner importance; it was part of himself.

And I was right. After we'd got to the top by way of a muddy slope, we spent a while – a very ears pricked while – looking over the corner of the field. It says a lot that neither of us would have had any idea of the amount of time involved. And the fact that so much time could be intently spent discussing changes in the soils, the lie of the land, and unspectacular fragmentary bits picked up really says the rest. He was so enthusiastic and enquiring, and I was soon under the spell myself.

We sat next to the cliff edge and painted pictures out of echoes, aware only of past damp and cold. The original inhabitants would have had such a view from their cliff-top settlement, intuitively sited to have the benefits of free-draining chalk and of the easefully fertile higher silts. As my companion pointed out, this was the furthest from (nearest to) the shallow flat bay, where one could have access to the shore at high as well as at low tide. And suitable easy access, judging by the slope we had come up. The bay, of course, would have been the southern end of the Wantsum, and the Stour estuary would then have been further up that channel. The exact topography was clearly given by the site of Richborough – Rutupiae – which we could just make out. This would have been on the mainland side of a constriction of the broad channel; the Stour would have come in to the front and to the left of it. Richborough with its ruined walls was more obviously one of the 'forts of the Saxon shore' put up to hold the line and police the waters in the face of barbarian pirates. But it had also been the bridgehead of the Roman invasion of Britain. There, where we looked, lines of trenches dug hastily against the shore had defended both men and boats; it was there that a triumphal arch was erected, where Watling Street symbolically started its way into the arteries of the coming province.

Richborough must have been all the more visible in Roman times from the site where we were, by day, and sometimes as a glimmer by night. As we knew from the coins, the inhabitants could have watched the traffic of the fort, of the Wantsum Channel, and of the larger Channel over the centuries of the Roman occupation – and beyond. But had they also been there, I wondered, to anticipate, to see, and to try to counter the Invasion. Were these among the shocked and scurrying population at the point where the sword of Rome struck? Was the first frantic shout of horror-struck disbelief from the cliff-top where we sat?

I had not kept these thoughts to myself and I do not think I could lay total claim to them. Just as it had become obvious in an unsaid way that some of the objects other than coins must throw more light on the site, so too it was clear that they might give an indication of pre-Roman occupation. Unbidden, and at the point of time where the cold and dampness became felt, James said that I really must look at all the 'stuff' that he'd collected. It was at his home. Would I come?

VI

Thus far, I have forgotten to mention my own name and it is inconsistent with what I am doing to be intentionally shy about this. It just seems 'off' to write something in the first person – often like a letter or journal – and then to put 'My name is Jonathan Riley'; but there it is. What brought this to mind was the walk back from Pegwell that day when it became the case that James and I got onto first-name terms.

Looking at other things from the site was only one part of the game, I knew that. He had been thoroughly chewed-off by his parents about how 'all the police business' had embarrassed them and how 'he should give them some thought'. His growing collection of objects at large – which he had somehow (and for some reason) kept quiet about – came to notice and was dismisssed as 'a load of dirty rubbish' which 'he shouldn't be wasting his time with'. His mother wouldn't have it in the house and it was all he could do to get a place of safekeeping, under sufferance, in the garden shed.

The house as we approached it didn't hold any surprises for me, I don't know why. I don't think I had actually been on a housing development so recently built, but I had certainly cleared plenty of land in advance of their construction, and I suppose I was familiar with the characteristics of layout and design. I could see, in an amused way, the craft of players in the development team. How the road wound to give shape, to deformalize, to make foci; how the largest of the houses were more forward and central; how the designs varied, mainly in combinations of small ways of finish, to give individuality; how each was detached, but so close to its neighbour; how the houses were positioned to the back of their plots, and how there was a splattering of designs with gables forward, to minimize frontage taken up; how an illusion of parkland space was created by an absence of fences, but how a good-sized park bench would look visibly out of scale.

Though it was a bit damp, cold and dark for any of them to be out, it was clear that the occupants had taken the ethos for their own and were busily applying it at the level of their individual properties. It's amazing how much DIY can go into houses that are ready to move into, a little bit here, a little bit there – a lot of it ready-made adult Lego – personal touches in blister packs. 'But, of course, the garden's the big thing when you move into a new house' – I wondered how many times that remark had been, and would be, wheeled out. I also wondered cynically if leaving (or making) the garden a challenge wasn't a rather good ploy. Happy the man who had a tree bole under a now flat lawn and the woman who found stones where topsoil should have been, for their struggle is ever green in the telling and their possession a joy. I looked at the juxtaposition of fish ponds, miniature trees, flower beds, and lawns – illusions of space within an illusion of space – and even wondered if the challenge was graded so as to give satisfaction but so as not to be beyond ability. I had heard such houses didn't sell well the second time round and thought it was because some people have to have things 'new', but I could now see a bizarre analogy with a made-up plastic model which had been marked as 'medium hard' – such pride of possession is impossible to transfer.

If I was feeling cynical James wasn't, and I came back to the here and now with a hint of guilt feeling. He'd obviously noticed that my thoughts had wandered off and I perhaps imagined signs of anxiety. I wondered if he was concerned about what I would think of where he lived, or of his parents. Alternatively, I thought he might be worried about what they would make of me, of what I did. I wasn't in any way convinced that it was either. I also considered whether a discrepancy between the two worlds was coming through but he was still in that state of naivety – which some never leave – where there is implicit belief that all the bits belong to the same jigsaw, and that it is complete.

Well, his parents made me very welcome. They berated their offspring for having given no warning; were obviously pleased that their home was just as they would wish it to be found (Mrs Stone tidied a few newspapers); and I was soon settled in a 'best room' atmosphere while parts of a tea set were being taken from its display case.

It struck me at the time as being reminiscent of being descended upon by the vicar and the more I have thought about it since, the more I appreciate that my first instincts were correct. I had been immediately assigned to that group of people – doctors, teachers, clergymen, and the like – who are a part of, but separate from, the lives of the majority. I was one of those 'others' and it gave me the cue for how I was going to play things.

There had already been introductions between the front door and the living-room along the lines of, 'Ted Stone, pleased to meet you.' (Shake of hands.) 'My wife Cathy. And, of course, our son James.' James had introduced me – 'Mum,' (and then 'Dad') 'this is the archaeologist I talked about,' the repetition preceded by a terminal click for the Saturday sport. I thought I should elaborate and I waxed on for a few sentences about archaeology and Cambridge, the fact that I had grown up in Ramsgate. It was only at that point that it dawned on me that 'Ted' and 'Cathy' must have been pretty well my contemporaries. I instantly pushed this to one side in my mind and I don't think there was the slightest interruption in what I was saying. Just as Cathy came through from the kitchen I concluded, 'and so, naturally, I'm interested in the archaeological site your son discovered – and in the objects which he tells me he has here.'

Ted said, 'Oh yes, he's got quite a sizeable collection. Haven't you, James? I dare say he's got quite a few things in it that are well worth having.'

Cathy had put her tray squarely on the occasional table and was now seated and leaning over. 'Yes, James, go and get some of that stuff to show Mr Riley. Would you like some tea Mr Riley, and a cake, only packet ones I'm afraid but it's not worth making your own these days. You do take sugar. Go along then, James, don't keep Mr Riley waiting.'

'They might make a mess in here,' responded James.

'Don't be silly.' She looked at me. 'Just put the wipe-clean tablecloth on the big table, you know, the one we keep.'

'Wouldn't it be best if Jonathan – Mr Riley – and I went out to the shed?'

'There isn't a light out there, is there, James?' his father said patiently. 'And besides it's cold.'

James went and I was left with Ted and Cathy, amused to think of them by those names. For all I tried I couldn't place them in my own schooldays but in those times a different school, or a different year, or a different form, are lands apart. But there they were, in front of me, and I could imagine. He had less hair than he would have had, she more perm; both sagged and had an air of being slightly worn. Other than that, one could have taken them out of the casual styles that had matured with their generation and put them, to effect, back into uniform. But that was just the externals, the shell, the packaging, though – whatever the adage says – it told sufficiently of what was inside. They were locals through and through in the most restricted sense. What one would accept in a nineteenth-century or earlier context in remote situations but which is, to some extent, universal – a self-seeding and extremely resistant parochialism of the mind.

'We're very interested in this history business, aren't we, Cath?'

'Oh yes, very. There's a lot of old things around, aren't there?' She looked at me.

'We see a lot on the telly, of course, very popular these days. Documentaries. You ever do anything in Egypt or Greece, Mr Riley?'

'No, no, Ted, I just do British archaeology,' I replied. He looked bemused.

'James seems very interested in that,' I continued. 'I'm sure you must be terribly pleased.'

'Of course we are, aren't we Ted?'

'Yes, Cath, that's right, Mr Riley. There's not a lot of really big archaeology round here but it's nice for the lad to have a hobby. Gets him out.'

'So long as it doesn't interfere with his schoolwork we don't mind, do we, Ted? I mean he's got to get an education to get a job.'

'No, but I must say I wish he'd look for the coins and what have you somewhere other than on a farmer's land. We had the police here, you know.' Ted said this as though it was just the sort of thing he could easily cope with at a personal level.

Cathy started to say something, 'Ted, . . .'

'Well,' I responded, 'you can't expect a local bobby to understand the importance of these things. He probably got a bit excited.'

Ted half agreed; Cathy began to look slightly worried.

'And I'm sure you're really very impressed with how clever your son has been.'

They both smiled in nervous and uncertain agreement as James, with an armful of boxes and tins, came in through the patio doors.

It was somewhat constraining looking at the stuff; Ted felt obliged to lean over and take an increasingly glassy-eyed interest; Cathy interrupting and fidgeting us continually in her helpfulness and offers of hospitality. I am not at my best in such situations; pulled one way by the need to concentrate and the other by distraction I am inclined to explode. But I told myself – with success – to take what was there for what it was and to keep playing the part.

Such collections tend to be a dog's breakfast, and this was no exception. James had not been able to resist bringing a selection of special treasures from here and there. It explained why I had heard footsteps overhead while he was supposedly outside. I quite liked the lead crest that had apparently fallen off the roof of St Lawrence church and which Brian claimed he had asked the vicar for. I also liked a piece of Bellarmine jar from the garden; the neck of an old soda-water bottle (presumably broken for the marble), through which a root had grown; a crude figured dagger, seemingly from the Malay archipelago; the carapace of a small turtle; and a number of fossils from a local coal mine.

While I was looking at these and lesser wonders I was also being fairly single-minded about isolating the material for the specific site and I ended up making James go outside more than once in order to get every last piece of it. Having established that it had not been kept by area of finding – except he knew the bits from the beach – I got his help to sort the lot by material and type of object. Next, I hived off the post-mediaeval bits and pieces – he was disappointed that a 'bone-cup' was actually what was left of a shaving brush – and then we were in a position to go through what was left. By and large it was Roman and, though unexceptionable, such stuff is really very accessible and I took the opportunity it offered to engage and involve the Stones. Simulating the assistance of James, I had them mentally reconstructing whole pots from parts of their profiles; looking at the detail on fine imported slipware; rubbing their fingers across the gritted interior surface of fragments of mortaria of presumed culinary use. They traced the lettering on the coins James had kept and wondered at the brooch fragments, early forerunners of the safety pin. While it lasted, it had all the charm of an engrossedly quiet, if small, primary school class. I suppose I had to point out that what was really interesting was that there was no brick, no stone, no tile.

Cathy made a face, Ted said, 'There you are, apart from that place next to the power station there's nothing much round here, and from what I've seen from the road there's very little of that.'

'But what's interesting,' I said pursuing my disadvantage, 'are the brooch and those pieces of black wheel-turned pottery. They could be just before or a bit after the Roman invasion but you see these fragments' – and I exhibited three small and fairly amorphous lumps of white-flecked red-brown pottery in the palm of my hand – 'these are definitely pre-Roman. The two together imply that there was a settlement there when the Romans came.'

James was excited at this rabbit having been pulled out of a hat but I wondered if he made the same as I did of me (or us) having well and truly lost the audience. There was much leave-taking and the meeting had clearly been a great success from all angles. In spite of promises to 'look in', that was that for the time being.

I feel obliged to point out here that the matter of the site did come to a good and satisfactory end. The finds, coins as well, were deposited in the County Museum; we covertly spiked the field with copper tacks and washers against further metal-detecting; and a brief note appeared in *Archaeologia Cantiana* under the names of Stone and Riley. I remember writing it, it started:

'Observation of a seasonal cliff-fall followed by *ad hoc* assessment through fieldwalking and selective metal-detecting within the ploughsoil horizon has established the existence of a hitherto unknown settlement of pre-conquest, Roman and sub-Roman date at Cliffsend near Ramsgate.'

PART TWO

VII

In many ways and for several months life then went back to a normal rhythm and round of events. But what am I talking about? The occurrences I have spoken of were not so different from those of my ordinary existence, except in retrospect, as running up to what came later. Life really started getting bizarre in an out-of-the-ordinary way when James (James from Ramsgate) turned up on my doorstep (my doorstep in Cambridge) one Saturday lunchtime. When I say my doorstep, I mean our doorstep, but I'm not going into that. I was washing up the dishes from the night before and from breakfast when I saw him hesitantly approaching. I opened the door, wiping my soapy hands on a tea towel, surprised, pleased and yet, even from the first, puzzled; we didn't get many personal callers, so it was a bit strange anyway.

I cheerily hoicked him in and assumed (said I hoped) he'd join us for lunch just as soon as I'd washed up enough things to eat it with. I introduced him in a casual and informal way; I involved him with the clutter of what was going on; and the ice seemed completely broken from the first instant. But, by the time we were sitting eating, I could see that my efforts had only been partially successful, for, at a deeper level, he was nonetheless experiencing some difficulty or culture shock. It must have been strange and disorientating for him really – just the lack of formal order; the fact that I was the one with the frying pan (of all things); the casualness; the odd and damaged furnishings, china and cutlery; the clutter of unaccustomed objects lying around, even untidiness. What was he meant to make of it? The house wasn't detached, it was small and there was no fitted carpet. Was this squalor? Was this poverty? Was it odd and not right? Had he been had? At the same time, he could see that much of what was around him was of his own inclinations writ large and made up of objects that were over the hill from pocket-money collectables. Together with the friendliness and informality he was also feeling constraints he didn't understand, not knowing what to do, beginning to feel himself out of place. I could see him getting into a vortex, going red, viewing his food strangely, starting to panic. Soon he would break or spill something, blow his nose on his napkin, run out. I knew what was happening – though not sure whether I was inside or outside the nightmare. I was careful to pull him to safety, to say that it must be different and odd but not to worry, to take it easy, that everything was fine, that there was no problem. I don't know whether there is a proper approach for such situations – I have my doubts – but for the parties involved and at that particular moment, it was the right thing and anxieties disappeared as suddenly as they had welled up. I quite purposely pre-empted the silence and lack of direction that might succour the return of the problem. At that instant I was aware of the turn of phrase and voice I had for Ramsgate; how out of place it was where I was; and what a curious thing it was there too. I wasn't quite sure where I was.

'What can we do for you then, James?' I asked, simply and directly.

His response was wordless, he just reached in his pocket and handed me a folded sheet of newspaper. I unfolded it; it was the front page of that Thursday's *East Kent Times*. The headline was 'FINDER KEEPS CLIFFSEND TREASURE' and next to it was a picture of a smiling youth showing objects in the palm of his hand, posed as only local paper photos can be. I read rapidly. It appeared that this Greg Philby had found no less than thirty silver coins of 'the Roman Emperor CLOALBIN AVG' (sic) together with a ring, using a metal-detector on the shore under our site ('reported in one of our previous issues'). He had handed the objects in to the police 'in case they were treasure trove' but 'to Greg's delight' the court had ruled that they were his because they 'could not be shown to have been hidden with intent to recover' and because they 'were found between high and low water mark'. It was portrayed as a victory for a local pools-winner-cum-adventurer over the powers-that-be and one was left to draw one's own conclusions regarding the fact that the farmer said that the treasure had probably fallen from his land ('which is eroding without protection'). The report made much of what a representative of the British Museum had said, quoting phrases such as 'a find of great and more than monetary importance' and 'cultural heritage', before pointing out with smug pleasure 'but the law says it all belongs to Greg'. As for 'lucky' Greg, he didn't know what it was all worth – though he expected it was a lot – and he was taking advice. The paper, aware that readers like such 'facts', revealed that an 'expert' they had contacted had said that with such coins in 'perfect condition' one could be talking about 'a five-figure sum'.

I wasn't altogether sure what response James wanted and the truth is that I was more than a little bit thunderstruck on my own account. By coincidence, I had been looking into the coinage and known history of Clodius Albinus (to get the name straight) in some detail on account of a very unusual coin which I had bought from a dealer. I was greatly excited.

'Do you know who this guy was?' I asked James.

He shook his head.

'After the mad Commodus was murdered at the end of the second century there were struggles over the succession – like there were after Nero's death. Someone called Pertinax was put up by the murderers, but he was quickly killed by the Praetorian guard, and they then quite literally auctioned the title and their loyalty – the highest bidder being one Didius Julianus. The outrage of Rome was soon transmitted to the provinces but, unfortunately, not one but three champions stepped forward: Pescennius Niger, governor of Syria; Septimius Severus, governor of Pannonia; and Clodius Albinus, governor of Britain. Briefly, what happened is that Septimius Severus declared Clodius Albinus his Caesar (deputy) and allied with him until Didius Julianus and Pescennius Niger had been dealt with; he, Septimius Severus, then turned on Clodius Albinus, declaring him a public enemy. Clodius Albinus' troops elected him Emperor (Augustus) in response but he (and they) were defeated in Gaul, at Lyons, and that was that. Clodius Albinus wasn't really British – he was born in north Africa – but he was the nearest we got to providing an emperor – for the whole Empire, that is – a bit like having an English Pope.'

'But the thing is,' I rolled on, well fired up, 'coins of Clodius Albinus are pretty rare. Wait a minute.'

I got up from the table and returned with a Roman coin catalogue, thumbing through to the correct page.

'Yes, look here, they're talking about a couple of hundred pounds for a denarius in circulated condition. Local papers aren't that accurate or on the ball, but there must be at least one since they've innocently quoted the obverse legend so accurately. Ah,' I said, turning the page, 'and that one was of him as Augustus, even more expensive – two hundred and fifty pounds. I suppose there is just one – but even that's remarkable – there could be more. It says they're in "perfect condition". Have you seen them?' I asked.

James shook his head, he was looking less enthusiastic and happy than he might.

'Look,' I said, 'I know how you feel. It was the site you found, that you did so much work with. I do know how you feel, it's happened to me. But it was there before you found it and one hopes it will be there for ever now, unless it's destroyed or completely excavated. I do know how you feel, believe me. But it would scarcely have been better if these coins hadn't been found – if you think about it. And besides, this Greg Philby,' I said, looking at the paper, 'is only interested in the money; we could still make something of the find from the archaeological point of view – this must be the first hoard of Clodius Albinus coins ever. Do you know the person who found them?' I asked, and then thought aloud, 'Good God, what happens if he sells them? We've got to get down there.'

James was oddly listless; our going down solved the problem of him getting home; my father was as semi-enthusiastic as ever about an imminent visit; and I suppose I was fevered – that seems the best way of describing it.

I basically just grabbed a few things – like change and keys – and rushed the two of us towards the car; the meal could hardly be said to have ended, it was more that it had been interrupted. And then we had to make a detour, a dash to my office for camera equipment. My mind, I remember, was working overtime and – as usual in such circumstances – I was thinking aloud. I have the (I suppose) irritating habit of suddenly getting emotionally and enthusiastically involved about something and then going over and over the matter with anyone who will listen, re-running events that have already occurred and positing all sorts of scenarios and eventualities. As we drove along James continued to be quiet, even evasive of involvement, and while I told myself he was fed up and probably tired, I began to feel pretty irritated. I had to say something, I was beginning to boil over.

'Look, James, I understand how vexing it must be that someone else found this stuff at "your" site but you've got to get a grip on yourself. In many ways, it's very exciting and there's things to be done. That's why you came across, isn't it? You can't complain that we haven't made a prompt start.'

I'm not sure whether he was looking at the glove compartment or the back of the tax disc but what he said, clearly, quietly, and mechanically, was, 'The point is, Jonathan, that the coins didn't come from the site.'

His words hung in the air. They threw me – I was mentally wrongfooted, if that's at all possible. We were about to pass the only real stopping place on the route and so I automatically went off on the sliproad, negotiated the roundabout, and parked in the lay-by. An AA man looked out from a portakabin-like shop/information centre the organization has there; I wondered vaguely whether I ought to ask for that year's handbook. This reminded me that the last time I'd been there I'd been as decisive about asking for the previous year's; that had been when my mother had died.

'I think you should explain a bit further, James,' I said, 'I could try guessing but . . .'

'The stuff in the newspaper's not from the site. That's important, isn't it? Isn't it as important as knowing what *has* come from the site?'

If my thinking had dislocated, this appeal made it click back. 'So why does the newspaper say what it does?'

'Because,' he said, 'the stuff was planted there – or more accurately, it was made believe that it came from there.'

'But why?' I asked incredulously. 'Why on earth would anyone do that? This Greg Philby?'

'Because it's a known site and because they'd thought up the wheeze about the shore next to it. It paid off.'

Information was not exactly freely flowing, but I made the most of what I had. 'So what you're telling me is that your site, a loophole in the law, and the coroner's court, have been used to launder these antiquities from somewhere else.' I'm not even sure I waited for him to nod. 'It's a bit improbably sophisticated, isn't it? Someone who can think up something as devious as that could, I am sure, just sell the stuff. The antiquities market isn't exactly as pure as the driven snow.'

'It was because Greg Philby's mother made him go to the police. His father's always in trouble, and she's sensitive about it. She found the stuff in Greg's room and he came out with it having come from the site – they'd decided on that – the bit about the shore was thought up later.'

'So who's "they", James? Where did the coins and the ring really come from? How do you know?'

He didn't want to say, full stop, and this brought me up short against how limited our relationship was. The only real point of contact was the site; he had found it difficult to justify intruding on me to tell me something that *wasn't* about the site; he now clearly thought I was intruding in asking him what it *was* about. One way or another I was fed up, perhaps it showed, perhaps it didn't, but I went off for a short walk to the garage up the perilously busy road to buy some jelly beans. It's funny the things one does.

VIII

I was in an increasingly flaming mood on the way up to the garage, and such trivial aspects of the world as presented themselves were all hateful and wrong. I don't like being thwarted; it throws me into a red-hot fog of confusion. I put two fingers up to some ass who hooted as he drove past and the disinterested attendant whose thoughts, if she had any, were somewhere else, angered me to snappy comment. When this happens I am totally within, and consumed by, the fire which I myself generate; I do not direct, my hands are not on the steering wheel. There is, however – and this is an outside view – always some strange alchemy in the situation, some transmutation whereby the cooling alembic is found to contain clarity and resolve.

By the time I was most of the way back to the car I was quite clear in my own mind. If this James didn't want to tell me what he didn't want to tell me then that was fine: I was not the police; nor an agony aunt; his best friend; his colleague; a pillar of virtue; or a crusading angel. If the coins and the ring were a cache then the odds were that it didn't matter where they came from – since 'buried treasure' doesn't usually have much of a context and it wouldn't have been from very far away, given the circumstances. Though the stuff didn't come from the site at Cliffsend, I was specially and personally interested because of the coin (or coins) of Clodius Albinus. What I had to do was quickly to find this Greg Philby; give him a bit of a pep talk; but make sure that I got some notes and photographs in case the material disappeared off the scene. I left it open in my mind whether and when I'd get in contact with one of the museums – they did know about it. As for James, I would tell him that I was still going to record the coins and that he needn't worry or be involved since my father could have seen it in the paper and told me about it. For, of course, he must have seen it.

I remember, I was psyched up when I got into the driving seat and, perhaps fatefully, prefaced what I was going to say with some banter about the sweets, which I put between us. James must have thought

I'd abruptly left him on his own to think about life. I hadn't – I hadn't thought of it – but I may as well have.

'I'm going to tell you what I know,' he said – 'I'd intended to anyway.'

He had intended to actually, he'd just lost his nerve. And he hadn't really come to see me to say where the coins weren't from; that wasn't what was worrying him.

'You know those East India Company coins you found in the hedge?' he asked.

'Yes,' I said, remembering them and wondering if this wasn't something of a diversion.

'Well, we put them there – Brian, Peter and I. Paul wasn't anything to do with it.'

'Right,' I said. It was interesting, and it's always pleasing when something clicks into place, but I still wished he'd get to the point.

'And do you know the old house on the West Cliff? The one that's just been left locked up for years, that's all overgrown and abandoned?'

'Oh yes,' I said – that house, did I know it!

'That's where we got them from.'

I looked at him, I felt in my heart a rather big clicking into place, but I said nothing.

'Oh, we didn't do anything bad,' he continued, '– too chicken! Brian knew that Greg Philby and some of his mates had broken in there and nicked a load of Indian stuff – swords and the like. So we went down there on our bikes one night – all tough. When we got there Peter just wanted to go home and hung around outside while as far as Brian and I got was to knock on the door, check if anyone was in – that was his idea. If there was going to be an answer we didn't wait for it, we ran. But those Indian coins, Peter saw them scattered in the drive by the light of his bike lamp. He wouldn't get off to get them, but Brian and I ran back in. We scarpered up the road after Peter as quick as we could, but when we all looked at the coins they didn't look much, Peter was scared of having them, and we hid them in the hedge.'

'So you never went into the house?' I enquired. This was partly for want of something to say, but also because that house had always seemed so tantalisingly mysterious to me from the outside and here I suddenly had a link with the inside of it.

'No,' said James; it was a reflex action to say that he had done nothing illicit. 'And,' he continued 'it was just as well because the police put two and two together about where all the Indian things being offered to dealers had come from. It wasn't the first time the place had been broken into. There's something odd about it, you see, it's just deserted. Anyway, the police apparently checked it was sealed up and then kept an eye out. No connection was made between Greg Philby and his friends and what had been stolen, but you can understand what a scare there was and why those coins stayed where they were in the hedge. Though,' he added, 'it's possible that Brian may have tried to sell them and put them back. You can never quite tell with him.'

My, this was fascinating. I'd always heard that the house had just been left as it was, with everything in it. I also vaguely remember – though I didn't know any details – that it was periodically broken into. The place was generally regarded as a nuisance, in an unquestioning way; it was scruffy, overgrown, falling to bits; those who clucked said no rates were paid on it; and the local constabulary were left with the thankless and hopeless task of trying to arrest a natural process of decay and depredation. I had always been as curious about what was in that house as Pandora might have been, and the coins and objects – no doubt including the dagger I'd seen – really rekindled the fascination and whetted my appetite. I wanted to know more.

'Has Brian been in there?' I hazarded.

'He hints at it,' said James, 'but I think it's talk. I think he knows what he knows from Greg.'

Greg! My word, I'd become so engrossed in the old house that I'd forgotten all about why we were where we were, in limbo halfway on a pell-mell journey from Cambridge to Ramsgate.

'James, James,' I said, repeating myself to stop the flow and start afresh. 'The Roman coins, the coins of Clodius Albinus. You remember? This is all very interesting, but what I want to know here and now is about them. That is, if you want to tell me.'

'I was getting there,' he remonstrated, 'the thing is that those coins came from the house too. They were stolen from there by Greg Philby, but the bit I don't understand is that they actually seem to have come from a tomb, there underneath the building. The building was put on top of it, or whatever. And there's other stuff. Greg Philby must have only taken what he thought was valuable. There's a skeleton,' – James said this by way of driving the point home – 'and pots and other things. It's very important – isn't it – and it's going to be ransacked and destroyed and looted to bits.'

All this was, for me, more than a little difficult to take in. Each twist and turn the existence and original provenance of this hoard of coins had taken – in the bare three or four hours I had known of it – had found me unprepared. To make matters worse, James was now very serious indeed; I didn't like to twitch for fear of pushing him over the brink, while I was equally aware of the perils of doing and saying nothing for more than a few seconds. To be honest, my reaction as it came through to me, was that what I was hearing was all just too fantastic. It was Ancient Egypt flavoured *Boys Own* stuff and I strongly suspected that the earnest James was the credulous believer of an embroidered story – and had probably been set up. But I couldn't say that.

'Good Lord!' was the best I came up with. 'How did you get to hear about this?' I immediately regretted adding, 'Brian?'

But he denied this. 'No, Brian doesn't seem to have known anything about the tomb, only the coins, and I haven't told him either.' James smiled. 'Peter's brother Paul is in the same class as Greg's little brother. It came out, but it's a big secret.'

'Sounds it,' I said. I was still very suspicious. Indeed, on the grounds that the simplest explanation is often the truth, I was fast coming to the conclusion that Greg Philby had found the hoard where he said he had and that James had been led up the garden path. 'And Brian only knows one half of the story?' I asked. I suppose I was trying to get him to question, without directly attacking, the main part of what he believed.

'Seems so,' he answered, 'and Peter and Paul know the other half.'

'And they've never got together?' I queried.

'Not after the metal-detecting at the site,' he explained. 'Peter and Paul's parents warned them off Brian.'

'And you?' I asked. 'Why did they tell you?'

'I wasn't meant to have told you that they had – please remember that – but they told me so that I'd tell you because they thought you'd sort it out. They didn't want you to know where I got it from because they don't want to be involved with the police again. That's OK?'

I added to my unspoken conclusion that he may have been the principal one being set up – but that he wasn't the only one. 'Surely,' I asked, 'if the police closed the place up after Greg Philby and his mates had been in there then they'd know about this tomb, if you get in from the house? I grant you they might not know the Clodius

Albinus coins came from there, but they'd know all about the tomb itself, wouldn't they?'

'It was found later,' James stated, 'after the house had been sealed up. It has a secret entrance.'

He knew I was doubting his story and the inkling of hurt I began to sense was as ominous as the chill that precedes a downpour. It was one of those situations that only worsen. I had inwardly winced at the mention of 'secret entrance' – the last shred of credibility vapourizing, as far as I was concerned – and coupled with the fact that I simply didn't believe it, was that I couldn't bring myself to care that I didn't believe it. I felt that I had been had once too often, I'd run out of whatever it is. Even as I started the engine, switched on the lights, and waited for the windows to clear, a quiet had established itself which was fully as pervasive as before we had turned off. I went back to feeling annoyed again and my assertion that 'it would be best to go for the coins first and think about the tomb later', though ostensibly kindly meant, was doubtless perceived as arch and dismissive. I suppose it was.

There are all kinds of silences and the one the rest of the way to Ramsgate wasn't of the comfortable sort. It was made worse, of course, by our being stuck in the car together but also, probably, by the knowledge that the end of the journey would impose its own resolution. It was actually at about the point that we were at that matters related to Ramsgate and my family always began to churn over in my mind – where we'd stopped hadn't helped – and so it was partly that I withdrew into this sphere of thought.

I did try to be cheery when I dropped James off, but after the long silence it was pretty hollow. He volunteered where I had to go the next day – 'Brisbane Avenue, the one with the purple GT with the broken suspension in the drive' – and it was tactily understood that I would be going alone. I leaned over to say that I'd let him know how I got on. He said, 'Good,' and closed the door, but he didn't move and I drove away leaving him at the kerb. He stayed standing there, I could see in the rear-view mirror.

Me, I was squaring up to seeing my father. I pulled into the drive, I rang the bell, the light went on in the hall, the door was unlocked and opened and there he was – benign, casual, cheerful, welcoming, interested. Have you ever considered how other people see the likes of your own father? It's a funny thought.

'Surprise, you phoning like that,' he said. 'Something up?'

Many would view this as parental care, only I would be jaundiced enough to spot the entire self-interest. He was concerned that something might have happened which would be a bother to him; he was never of help in adversity, seeing it only as an imposition upon himself.

I reassured him and then we quickly got into the familiar territory of some compilation of the following:

'You're early.'

'Didn't know when you were coming.'

'Have a good trip?'

'Which route did you take?'

'I've eaten; I'll put the kettle on and put something on the table for you.'

'I was watching the news.'

No real contact, but easier than real contact.

IX

The back end of the evening had also gone much as usual. That is, my father had grunted, 'There's a paper there if there's anything on you want to watch.' I'd looked and mentioned something inoffensive and the only thing halfway worth looking at. But it wouldn't have mattered what I'd said, he'd still have humphed, given the impression I was trying to be 'clever', and gone to bed early. I would have sat and watched whatever it was and whatever was on until I nodded off, then I would have carried that sleepiness carefully upstairs. The point is that that evening was no exception, there was nothing to 'go over' – to go over and over – in my mind about the coins, the site, James, the house, and what have you. The subject and I had exhausted each other and matters were worked through and non-problematic. There was the small gnawing prompted by my reason for coming. My father's comments ran along the lines of: 'missed that lot, didn't you?'; 'thought you'd finished there'; 'didn't think you'd be interested'; 'they sent someone proper down from one of the universities'. It was the perplexing usual that I still couldn't quite cope with.

I was up in time to take my father some tea in the morning but was otherwise kept hovering by the knowledge that it was Sunday. I'd calculated the time I could reasonably go up to Brisbane Avenue as about eleven – though I obviously didn't want to miss Greg Philby – and so I havered as well as hovered. I was fiddling with the small pile of free local newspapers and old holiday brochures that constituted a last ditch source of distraction when – at exactly nine – the doorbell went.

'Milkman,' my father pronounced. 'Could be the postman,' he added, lest he be wrong. 'Someone for you,' he called out, as though tolerant victim of a minor trick.

I went out in the hall – it was James. But my word, he was soaked, had chalk all over his coat, and was hollow-eyed and chattering-shattered – as though he'd spent the night in a ditch.

'Been down the site early?' I said; it was quick camouflage thinking. 'Come on through and have a cup of tea, but you'd best take your shoes off.'

I knew saying this would both please my father and make him disappear on the pretext of putting the kettle on. James put his shoes on the sheet of newspaper which was perennially in the hallway on the flowery fitted carpet, but he wouldn't part company with his coat and I thought this was as good a reason as any for guiding him through the patio doors of the living-room into the little kitform conservatory.

'I hope I haven't come too early,' James said, 'but I've been hanging around outside and it's freezing. I thought nine was OK.' We had both sat down in the folding chairs that were there.

'Fine, fine,' I said, 'but where have you been? To the site? Why at this hour? You fall down the cliff? What have you been up to?'

He eyed me with exhaustion, unbuttoned his coat, pulled up his jumper, put his left hand in under his right armpit, and produced – and handed me – a bone. 'Well?' – that's all he said.

In came my father with the tea, and some biscuits. 'That where you are! Bit cold for me out here. I'll go round and get a newspaper. Here, it's Sunday isn't it, blow me! There's more in the pot if you can be bothered to get up and get it.'

Tea was drunk – I even went and got a refill – and James ravenously ate his way through every last biscuit. But otherwise there was silence until the door went. It was my turn to pull the bone out, from by my chair where I'd propped it against the conservatory wall, and I rotated it in front of me, a hand at each end, and answered the question.

'Femur; left, I think; human; adult. Find a grave did you?' I asked.

'That's where you usually get things like that from, isn't it?' It wasn't simply cheek or exhaustion. 'Now do you believe about the tomb under the house?' He was looking straight at me, unsmiling. 'I went there last night, I got that from there as proof – if you believe me.'

He was proving his point – successfully: for me it was like belief being dependent on the shake of a kaleidoscope. What I had concluded was embarrassing, had now been capriciously transformed into a tremendously exciting source of anguish and interest.

'But you didn't disturb anything did you? You shouldn't really have brought this bone away, you know. How'd you get in there? What was it like?'

I was all fired-up, fresh; he was exhausted, his brain cold and slow-moving. I wondered if he was going to collapse into sleep just where he was.

'I went straight down yesterday evening; I didn't go home; my parents will have thought I was in Cambridge last night – see? Mind, I had to find a bike with a light left on it first – it wasn't much good – and I put it back this morning – the lamp, that is. How I got in was how I'd heard Greg had been in. It'd foxed the cops, but you know the window in the sloping garage roof at the side?'

I nodded, I did know.

He continued, 'It isn't a window, not with a frame, but it's built in the roof like, it's like glass where there could be tiles. And the thing is that you can push it, slide it, under the tiles above. Only a couple of foot, but enough. So I dropped in there, no problem.

''Course it was pitch black and the place was in a hell of a mess. I tell you I wanted to get out pretty quick. At first I couldn't see where you got into the tomb but when I got into the house I felt gritty stuff under my shoes and I stooped down and it was like crumbs of cement and brick.' He rubbed his fingers together in demonstration. 'There wasn't much, and I could have looked for ever, but I was suspicious about a bookcase that was up against the wall there. There were books in it,' he said, 'but some of them had been put in upside down.'

I was vastly impressed.

'I tried to shift the bookcase,' he continued, 'but I couldn't – not that is until I'd taken all the books out and stacked them. Christ it seemed like a long time, might have been nothing there, and I wanted to get out. But guess what, there was a hole behind – it'd been broken through – I don't know how Greg had found the place, I really don't, but he had and he'd swept the rubbish back into it. It was all neat and tidy from the outside, you could see nothing you see.'

'Go on, go on,' I said.

'The hole,' he continued, 'was about door width, but not very high, and I shone the light in and saw that you could drop down onto a flight of steps, going down steep, covered in rubble – couldn't see the bottom. I didn't fancy it, I tell you, but I knew I'd found what I was looking for so I went in feet first. It was cold and it was very quiet and I was scared enough of being found out in the house and now I was wondering what might be at the end of the steps – they were in a sort of tunnel, though it was a height you could walk in. I switched off the lamp – and I felt my way down – I don't know why – I was actually very scared and though I was trying to be silent it seemed I kept kicking bits of rubble down further. I don't know, I thought something was going to grab me and I got a real shock when I couldn't feel steps in front of me but I could still touch the walls on either side. They were of chalk, just like the cliffs. I suddenly imagined myself dropping into a shaft or something and I stayed where I was in the quiet just listening and not knowing what to do. There was nothing, absolutely nothing, just complete silence. In the end I couldn't stand it any longer and switched on the light – not that I could see much by it – but the tunnel was pretty much the same except that it was just sloping down now instead of going down steeply with steps. But the surprise was to come.'

'Come on then,' I said. I was quite literally on the edge of my seat.

'After going round a bend the tunnel came out into a chamber – it was as big as a room,' he was being emphatic and looking at me, with one hand raised to stress what he was saying, 'and wherever I shone the torch the walls and the ceiling were covered with sea shells stuck in patterns – just like Roman mosaics, all over. And the roof, it went up in the middle, you could hardly see the top, and there were like some benches carved in the chalk at the sides and there was an altar at the end – with shells just the same – and there were niches in the wall, big ones and tiny ones. Some place that, I tell you, the patterns of the shells! Jonathan,' he said, firmly underlining his reinstatement, 'it's some discovery you know – it really is! Even my mum and dad would be impressed,' he added, smiling.

I went to open my mouth, but James saw that and quickly responded by continuing his story. He was bursting to come out with it and was so tired I think he was frightened of not reaching the end. 'The stuff is there, well there was stuff in there but it didn't look much, but you have to use your imagination – well *you* know that. There were just bones and some smashed pottery that I could see – and I couldn't see a lot because of the bike-light. The pottery was like the pottery from the site, I'm sure of that,' he stated confidently, 'and there you have one of the bones. It was all a bit scattered across the floor, and I could only see it bit by bit, and I didn't want to disturb anything. I marked where that bone came from but someone had been in there recently and turned the place over. I found a fag end. We don't know what's gone.'

He had every right to look as pleased with himself as he did. As for me, I was flabbergasted. The adrenalin was running high, I wanted to get in there, I was worried about the tomb – including the coins from it. It was all so major, and then there was the problem of where it was, the legality of even knowing about it and things stolen. Personally I was fascinated, and professionally I scented a coup. I was pulled in all directions at once. I stood up, the bar across the front of the chair had, I could feel, been cutting into me, there wasn't room to pace up and down.

'I don't know what to say,' I said truthfully. 'James, this is all fantastic.'

'You believe me?' he said.

I nodded penitently, 'I believe you.'

'You want to see it?' he asked.

I was dreading that question coming as much as the thought of not seeing it. Both options were as bad as each other. How in heaven's name could I break into the house – me? There was a strange reversal of position, I was as chicken as James' erstwhile friend Paul. And anyway, could I encourage him to do what he'd done again – hadn't I enough to feel guilty about already in that direction?

James could see I was in turmoil and he smiled. 'There's no problem, no problem at all.' He yawned, looked pleased and amused, and slumped a little more.

I was frankly perplexed. 'No problem me strolling in there?'

'Almost,' he replied, managing to smile and keep his eyes open at the same time. 'When I was down in the tomb there was something about the air. It was the cigarette end that made me think of it. I mean the place didn't smell of cigarettes but then it didn't smell of nothing, it smelt a bit like it does in caves, fresh and, um, a bit like of the sea.'

He looked at me to check I knew what he was talking about. I did.

'I got up close to the end wall, but I couldn't check it over with the light because I was terrified of treading on anything while I was doing it. So I thought I'd look along the floor there just, make sure of what there was. And guess what? There was a big mouse hole, a sort of burrow through the wall near the right-hand corner. I put my hand down and I could feel a draught; I got down on all fours and put my nose to it – it was the smell of the sea I was talking about. But there is just the wall – I checked, I shone the light over the pattern of shells in the area and ran my hand over them. But there was the sea on the other side. I couldn't see anything through the hole. Do you know what I did?'

I shook my head in response.

'I got the other one of those bones,' he said, pointing, 'tied my handkerchief to the knob at the end and shoved it through the hole. By that time the bike-lamp was so dim I could just about make my way back to the passage I'd come in by, by holding it right against the floor. I felt my way up the stairs and pulled myself up at the house. Then I pushed the bookcase back and I put all the books back – exactly as they were, including the ones that were upside down. Then I . . .'

At which point he simply went to sleep, where he was, in mid sentence, head hanging forward. Exactly at the moment I heard my father coming in the front door! I tried to wake James but I couldn't. However I shook him, he settled down like a sack of vegetables, or a guy. He was dead to the world. And I was in a panic about it because of my father, and the certainty of his being as typically helpful and useful as ever. I headed him off before he got to the patio doors by going into the living-room and closing them behind me.

'What's going on?' he asked, disapprovingly, looking over my shoulder.

'Oh, he fell asleep while I was talking to him. He was up early. Best leave him be.' Ever tried making light of, or damping down, a subject when your mind is racing on something else?

'I suppose I could read my paper in here,' my father responded. 'Not in trouble, is he?'

'No, he's not,' I affirmed. 'I'll make you some tea.'

'Twice in one day! You OK?' he cracked, and sat down, pleased with himself.

It's difficult to explain why it was completely out of the question that I should leave James as he was and get up to Brisbane Avenue myself. But it was, and I had to sit there as subjects cropped up from the reading in hand. I was like a tethered goat with an unfortunate allergy to knowledge, wisdom and debate. My father's enjoyment was in seeming inverse proportion to my own, he was even bringing into play such fine phrases as 'course you wouldn't remember', 'those who work for a living', and 'people who think they're clever, like you'. It couldn't last for ever and I was brain-numbed and thankful when the clock struck twelve.

'I'll go and wake him up,' my father said. 'I've got to put the lunch on now.'

'I'll wake him up,' I put in, 'and don't bother about lunch. I've still got to go out today.'

'Thanks for telling me.' I had told him actually.

X

James was still groggy when I got him in the car, but he was awake – awake and feeling embarrassed.

'Sorry,' he said, 'I was just so tired.'

'Never mind,' I reassured him, 'it doesn't matter. Forget it. Look, I've got to get up to Brisbane Avenue to at least get some photographs. You'd best not come anyway, so I'll drop you off at your house. We'll make it that we've arrived from Cambridge this morning.'

'That's what my parents will have thought anyway,' James said.

'You'd better leave your coat in the car, but I don't know what you're going to do about your shoes, unless you do something now.'

'I'll just say we came by the site. It could be the case for all anyone knows.'

There wasn't much of Ramsgate to drive through and I wasn't wanting to dally unnecessarily before going on. I started the engine and got straight to the point of what was uppermost in my mind. 'Before you nodded off, James, you said there'd be no problem me seeing the tomb. How's that? I'm not saying you shouldn't have done what you did, but let's say that the thought of doing it myself is taking my mind off anything else being a problem.'

'That's right,' he laughed, 'I never told you. Where's the bone?' he asked with suddenness.

'It's in the boot with the camera equipment,' I said. 'Don't worry.'

'Come on, I want to show you something, drive down the "Chine". Have you got a torch?' He'd all of a sudden come to life.

'No, no,' I responded, 'there isn't time, there really isn't.'

'I want to show you, not tell you,' he insisted. 'Won't take five minutes, honest.'

I sensed there was a good chance he was going to be put out if I refused and I was still feeling contrite for having disbelieved him the evening before. Anyway, I was excited at any prospect of getting in or near the tomb and gave in. 'Five minutes you say! Down the "Chine".'

What the 'Chine' was, or is, takes a little explaining. I don't know where the idea originated from – China perhaps – but there were three manifestations in Ramsgate, the one on the 'West Cliff' was the one I knew and the one in question. It was an artificial defile cut from slightly inland down onto the 'esplanade' at the cliff base. I suppose it and the others were constructed when the town was a thriving resort with thinning crowds of strolling holiday-makers along its seaward edges. And I suppose that then the rock-effect sides could almost have seemed magical as one walked between the informally cascading semi-exotic greenery they were designed to be planted with. But by my time the illusion was laid bare, the 'rocks' one wasn't supposed to climb up contained hardened mud and little else, their sides, only too apparently, of rendered brick. As for the crazy-paved path – well, it had been made with the edge of a board pressed into the wet cement. The foundations of a ticket office, pivots for barriers, and posts for traffic lights were all that remained of a later desperate and failed scheme for letting non-existent hordes get to the beach by car. In the end it was unclear whether the blindly winding incline was for cars or pedestrians, but it mattered as little as parking restrictions in a deserted town.

Yes, we could go down the 'Chine'. And the prospect was all the more enticing when I realized we had to pass by the abandoned house James had been in the night before in order to get to it. In the event I couldn't see much of the house; by the time I'd picked out the window in the garage roof it was past, an undetailed mass behind an overgrown hedge. There was no chance of me stopping – and that wasn't because of being in a hurry. James looked straight ahead.

I negotiated my way down the 'Chine', meeting nothing; it was even more neglected and dismal than I remembered. At the bottom I turned left onto the deserted esplanade – a fine name for a straightforward work in concrete. Actually, there were three fishermen, or boys, in a spaced clump, and a man and dog walking the other way, duty done. But they were a way off from where James had me stop, which was below a Second World War 'gun emplacement' with broad steps up to it. We stood and looked out momentarily. I have put 'gun emplacement' in inverted commas because dummy guns – wooden barrels – were put there in order to fool the population into a feeling of readiness. Real guns – if there'd been any – would have caused the cliffs to collapse. The sea, as ever, was limpid, dull and opaque; an effect of the chalk. I was thinking of telling James about the guns while thinking, at the same time, that the high double arched hollow we were in had probably been built before, originally to remedy some fault in the cliff as far as supporting the promenade above went, though doubtless then used as a genteel look-out with benches. The place had its share of litter, and there were the remains of a fire in amongst the lumps of chalk that had been hurled against, or used to scrawl upon, the walls.

'Here,' James said.

I turned; he had climbed over the railings on one side and, while hanging on with one hand, was in the process of insinuating himself into a vertical crack between the edge of the 'gun emplacement' and the cliffs behind it. He disappeared, all but for a beckoning hand, and I followed and – to my surprise – managed to get myself through into where he had gone. I needed considerable physical help and guidance from the start but though it was, of course, dark, it was clear what was going on. The 'gun emplacement' had actually been built to block off the mouth of a cave, and what we had done was to get round the blocking and drop some fifteen feet down an improvised ramp of debris onto the cave floor. Where we had come through was now a narrow slit of light, the back of the 'gun emplacement' was an expanse of concrete with what remained of the wooden shuttering still in place, while beneath our feet was the coarse sand and flint nodules to be found in any cave around there. It wasn't like a normal cave though, it was dead and dusty with a shadow rather than a damp green dado upon the walls. It was chill.

James called me from further in; it wasn't so deep a cave – they aren't – and I could see that he was at the end of it, my eyes having adjusted by the time I reached him. There too, was a length of wrenched-off, rotten shuttering going up and into the cave roof, which was at no great height. It was a primitive ladder but it sufficed and I pulled myself up through the hole in the roof of the cave as through a trapdoor into a house attic, but here it was up into an otherwise blind corridor carved out of the chalk. We were not a very great distance along this when James held back and made me pass him with the torch. There, immediately ahead, the passage was blocked from floor to ceiling by a sturdy brick wall. As surprising in an ordinary way as everything else I'd seen, except that sticking out below the lowest course was the head of a human femur with a handkerchief tied to it.

'How on earth . . .,' I began to ask, bending down to the bone.

'Simple, it was just too simple,' James replied. 'I made that bloody hole. Brian and I and some others used to come down and fish on the West Cliff a few years back. We'd seen pigeons going in and out of the hole at the front and we took a look – it was a big adventure. We hadn't been the first up here, since that wood jammed against the wall was there, and I doubt if we've been the last. What we tried to do for a while was to get through this blockage here by digging under it. It was great fun with candles and that, but all we had to do it with was a bit of metal railing and our hands. It was just me and Brian that did it but he got bored and I came down on my own, managed to get the piece of metal through under the wall to the other side, and then got fed up myself. Little did I know, eh!'

'That's incredible,' I said. I was lost for words, but I was also thinking pretty hard about what I'd seen.

'So,' James continued, 'there's only that wall between you and the tomb. That's what I meant. Wouldn't take much shifting with some decent tools, would it?'

I put both bone and torch into my left hand and I ran my other one speculatingly over the face of the brickwork. 'No, it wouldn't take a lot,' I answered. 'I'd like to think about it. It was patterned with shells the other side, you say, and you couldn't actually see this passage?'

James made some sort of noise of assent. 'You can imagine what it was like here last night with no light at all. It was the very devil getting in through the front – I fell all the way down, almost, and then I had to get up through the roof and crawl along in the pitch black. It was great feeling the bone and the handkerchief, just great but I didn't have anywhere to go then, and, anyway, I didn't dare crawl back along to the drop to the cave when there was no torch and there would be no light coming in from the outside. I just went to sleep here against the wall.'

'Well,' I said, 'you've had a busy day – let's get out of here.' He was visibly bushed by the time we did, probably worse than before; he'd all but fallen down from the cave roof and had to be virtually hauled up into the outside world. I had to laugh while I was opening the car boot, I looked at James and then at what I could see of myself. There wasn't much to choose between us as far as the state of our clothes went. As for the bone, it was the partner of the other one, but then there wasn't any reason why it shouldn't have been.

Time was ticking on; James' answer that it was twenty to two only confirmed my worries. A sense of panic and urgency was fast upon me as it had been upon James the day before. I wished I knew what to do: it's terrible being in a frenzy and, at the same time, directionless. I was still determinedly going to see the coins – but that was as much of a first step as had been James setting out to see me. What next? And as to the importance of it all: well, in my heart it felt fantastic, the sort of discovery that is so amazing that one cannot admit that it could occur and, even if it did, couldn't imagine someone like oneself having a part in it. I'm always a bit like that, but I remember at that moment setting myself against any doubts that might come into my mind – I would uproot them, deny them existence. And I also decided that I was going to see the matter through – I didn't know how, but for me this was the big one, and I was going to square up to it. I was very resolute and I'd already put whatever end there might be above whatever means might be necessary to reach it.

James had nodded off on the way up the 'Chine' – and a good job too. Given the situation, my thoughts on ruthlessness, and him held upright in the passenger seat, it was no wonder I flushed cold on seeing a police panda car parked outside the deserted house. The garage drive gates were open – I reckoned the small gate couldn't have been operational – and there were two policemen with peaked hats poking around the outside of the building. I drove past, but I had to see what was going on so I went to the next access across the boulevard, came back round, and parked a little way up. By that stage they'd finished pulling at the doors and checking windows and I thought they were going. They were, but one of them stopped at the garage and climbed up and walked along the wall beside it. It looked quite an improper thing to do in a suit of clothes, in an official capacity. But he'd sussed about the window in the garage roof. He looked at it from close to, didn't touch it, just looked and, saying something to his mate, jumped down. They closed the gates behind them and drove off.

I drove off too. This was another twist – and a worrying one. Apart from anything else, I wondered how the devil they knew anyone had been in there. It restored one's faith in the forces of law and order – just at the wrong time – but it was, nevertheless, a mystery. Perhaps some sleepless neighbour, but the house simply wasn't overlooked.

I decided not to tell James for now, shoehorned him out of the car at his house to fare as best he could, and drove on.

XI

Brisbane Avenue brought back memories. I'd had a girlfriend who lived there when I was not very much older than James was then. She was my first, really – both girlfriend and soulmate – and I thought how very fond I was of her still in long retrospect. We were both local but looking out; when we went it was separate ways, but only after having been of great mutual support in the preparation. I'd never seen her since.

A random crosscurrent of thought made me realize for the first time the strangeness of the elements of a whole planned and built council estate having been named after places in Australia. Formerly this phenomenon had seemed as normal as, say, telephone boxes being red. And Brisbane Avenue had changed: it was older, I was older, and I suppose both it and I had developed parts with a self-conscious pride of ownership that one could see as such by contrast, if in that sort of mood.

As for the house I was looking for, that was easy to find. There was no mistaking a purple GT in the drive, decaying where it sagged, mould starting in the window sockets, tyres flattening, tax disc two years out of date. Even so, it was where pride had been; what else I could see was lived in with neglect. The garden wall had been half knocked down to admit the car, and the rubble still lay where it had been piled; the garden was more threadbare than wild and had an old sofa and some carpet in it; the house itself was unkempt, the number daubed in paint on the wall.

The odour came over me as soon as the door opened. It was anticipated and was as unnoticed as when one looks into the face of someone disfigured.

'Mrs Philby?' I enquired.

She looked at me with a weary sort of resignation and made some slight noise or gesture of assent.

'Well, it was your son Greg I wanted to see, actually. Is he in?'

There was a scarcely perceptible change in the look in her eyes, but it was still one of resignation. The slight noise or gesture was in the negative. She would have liked to have been able to close the door but thought better of it and made a move to meet the situation.

'What do you want of him?' she asked.

'I read in the paper about the Roman coins he found and I wanted to see him about them,' I said.

'So you're not from the police, the social, or the probation? You the farmer?' she queried, less rhetorically.

I shook my head.

'Well it's a pity he's not in,' she said.

'It is,' I replied, 'I've come a long way.'

'A long way, eh?' There was clearly something going on in her mind. 'Don't think he's gone out for long, you could come back.' Then she thought further. 'Dare say you might be wanting to have a look at those coins. I don't think Greg'll be long. You'd best come in. Place is a mess but what the hell.'

It was a mess too. She took and lit a cigarette before clearing a chair of washing for me. I expect her need for the weed had helped her thinking along but she clearly wanted to keep me all the same.

'Oh I didn't offer you a fag, I'm sorry, so many people these days don't, do they?' She proffered the packet.

I held up my hand and smiled graciously, giving no offence.

'There's a drink,' she said, 'some sherry. I don't usually at this time of day you understand, but being Sunday after dinner.'

'I won't stop you getting on with your drink, Mrs Philby – and I must apologize for having turned up like this on a Sunday afternoon. It's very kind of you. A cup of tea would be nice.'

She called from the kitchen as she was making it. 'You only just missed Greg you know, he went out after dinner.'

I cursed to myself, but then, wasn't I actually better off? As I sat and thought about it I looked around. It was the sort of place where everything is cheap, in disorder, in bad taste, run-down and – in a nutshell – it was pretty pigging. They'd evidently had their dinner sitting watching the television – three plates with the red-smeared remains of something fried lay abandoned. There were a lot of magazines and papers around and clothes, some of which were no doubt clean washing. But it wasn't as though what was seen was the aberrant abuse of teenagers left for a weekend, something that would disappear with a good tidy. No, it had real depth and maturity which had crusted and discoloured at the edges. I wondered about the date of the bottom newspaper of the pile in the corner and whether the person who'd left the broken skateboard under the telly was now well beyond such things. I'm undoubtedly overdrawing it but the flavour's right, even if too strong. And I also thought how astonishing it was to be sitting in a house – at least, a part of one – where nothing that caught the eye would have had any resale value at all. If the inhabitants of the house had disappeared, the whole contents would have probably ended in the corporation tip.

Mrs Philby came in with two mugs of tea and set them down between us. If she broke the train of my thought she also set a hare for new ones, for she was a kindly looking individual – I think careworn is the best adjective I can come up with. I had the strong impression that she wasn't the sort to be pressed down simply by poverty and squalor; if she hadn't had the cares she would have been happy – and undoubtedly had been. The image came to me of once, when I was feeling particularly oppressed by stress at work and by money cares – of once having looked through an old shop window, through a crack in curtains that had been put across it. There inside was squalor, a fire of scrap wood in the grate, on the occasional table in front of it sliced bread spread with margarine and jam, a big teapot and mugs, and four people sitting round. And my God those people looked happy. That's the end of the image and, do you know, I was in echo momentarily happy that the mug Mrs Philby gave me was none too clean and that the sole teaspoon on offer was caked with sugar.

She was actually more urgent than I was, but only because she thought she'd delayed as long as she might. I couldn't quite believe it when she picked a tea caddy off the mantlepiece, opened and upended it. The coins came out in a pile with a rather upsetting clunk; with them was a scattering of two-inch-square white paper, coin envelopes.

'They were in the envelopes, like, when he got them back but it says the same blamed thing on each one so there didn't seem any point. Anyway Greg likes to hold them in his hand.'

I smiled in, I suppose, a rather dazed way. They were indeed silver denarii and, from what I could see, they were all of Clodius Albinus and in mint condition. No matter how much the idea of raw treasure had been sophisticated out of me, those particular coins still made me feel a bit weak; I merely said, 'May I?'

The first thing I picked up were the envelopes, sifting the remaining coins from between them. Mrs Philby was quite right, on each was written in neat, blue biro, round hand 'CLO ALBIN AVG Denarius', this was unvarying, mechanical. The coins I laid out in three lines of ten, all face up, head to the right. They were irregular, as early coins are, but they were also – as I have said – in absolutely mint condition, and it even looked as though the only marks on them might have been caused recently by being jiggled around in a pocket – or the tea caddy. I smelt a rat and I took the jeweller's glass I'd brought out of my pocket and inserted it in my eye. The features on the portraits were completely unrubbed, the coins were to all intents and purposes almost as good as new. But I saw there was more to it than that as I compared one with another – they were all made from the same die. I could see this in each stroke of the lettering and the distances between them; it was apparent in the locks of the hair, the form of the eye; it was completely obvious and unmistakeable. Moreover, in the course of this examination, I'd checked and found all the reverses were the same; again, not similar, but identical.

This had me floored; I hadn't been expecting it. I'd heard of a new breed of hardened plastic dies; I knew there was a magazine devoted to publishing details of modern forgeries of ancient coins. I wondered if the laundering wasn't laundering of another nature. But then, why were the coins sitting in front of me? What was it all about? I was flummoxed and, once more, caught unprepared.

'And then there's this,' Mrs Philby said. With overcome hesitation, she put her hand in her apron pocket and produced – the ring. 'Greg wanted me to have it . . . he's a good boy . . . but, well.'

There are some rings which are so very impressive, like those of an archbishop or of a monarch. They are rings above rings, and this was one of them. I instinctively handled it with considerable reverence – and, ironically, it had been the element of the find I had been most prone to forget. It was massive, rounded, worked smooth gold, not a piece of drawn, chopped off tubing, and the bezel was inset with another coin – gold but, as far as I could see, otherwise identical to the silver ones. Breathtaking. I began to suspect that I wasn't among forgeries but among objects of such quality and rarity that I was equally unfamiliar with them.

I looked across at Mrs Philby; she filled the void more quickly than I was able to. 'I'm sure Greg will be back soon,' she said, looking at the electric clock next to where the tea caddy had been. 'They are very nice, and with you having come such a long way.'

I focused on the clock too in pretended interest, thinking quickly.

'I'd like to wait, but time is getting on and, to tell you the truth, I was a bit delayed getting here, which makes it all the more annoying that I missed Greg. I think in case he doesn't come back soon I'd better take a photograph so that I can write to him, or telephone him. Don't you?' I knew there wasn't a telephone. 'I have a camera in my car.'

The suggestion brought unqualified relief to Mrs Philby, fearful as she was that I might go. Her idea of taking a photograph obviously didn't extend beyond a holiday snap but, while the clutter I brought in left her bemused, it was welcome for the time that she thought the process was going to take. Not that what I had was anything but simple, and not that what I was going to do with it would take very long. The device was something I had rigged up for the specific purpose of photographing coins and it consisted of a stand with two attached floodlights on bendy arms, a camera with a macro lens at the top, a white matt board at the base, and a shelf of non-reflective glass between. It was set on the occasional table in a twinkling, plugged in, and the coins carefully arranged, with a scale symmetrically in pattern. Mrs Philby gasped when the lights went on; I checked the exposure against neutral grey card, removed it, re-checked the focus against the scale, and then pressed the cable to set the time release going. The routine was much practised and it was seconds before I had turned the coins over, marked the displacement of the dies, taken another shot, and then laid them quickly but carefully aside in the same pattern. Next, I set the ring up, using Blu-Tak, and took a shot of it both in plan and of the bezel. Thoroughly in the swing of things, I went back over the coins taking close-ups of a few.

The gimcrackery had left Greg's mother quiet – perhaps even stupefied – and she watched on as I plugged in a small electronic balance and weighed each coin from the pattern, noting down $A1 \ldots A2 \ldots A3 \ldots$ in grammes. Similarly, I rubbed the edge of each coin down a piece of paper, putting the identifying number below the streak produced – this, as I explained, was to enable the metallic content to be analysed.

Whatever happened, I did now have a record and I felt the easier for it. I still had my anxieties and ill-defined ambition, but I had gained some ground I couldn't lose. I was quite confident about the photographs; I had got taking them down to a fine art. Then I took the equipment out to lock it in the car boot but brought the camera itself back in as though I had had second thoughts. The truth is that I had rewound the film, taken it out, and substituted another, which I advanced the right number of frames; this subterfuge had no purpose, but I remember doing it. The stuff was still on the table; the leg bones – which I'd been looking at – were in the boot of the car. Those coins and the ring before me weren't mere objects or treasure; those legs were once attached to the same body that had a finger that wore the ring. In archaeology it is a question which is as rarely warranted as it is beset with pitfalls, but it entered my mind and wouldn't go away. The question was simply 'Who?'

XII

There was a silence when I got back into Mrs Philby's house. The business had been done – what I primarily came for, and what she had clutched onto to delay my departure. I had said that I had to go, and she didn't know what to say. I sat on the side of an armchair, car keys in hand. She wanted to say something, I guessed it was about money; in a way I guessed right.

'It's a bit like winning the pools when you've never entered them, if you see me,' she opened. 'Money never come so easy in my time, leastways not in a way that doesn't bring trouble, and I don't trust it when it does. It don't seem right somehow, I thought you was from the police or something,' she gave a little laugh and smiled in the ghost of a girlish way. 'I suppose I just expect trouble.'

It wasn't what I'd anticipated. She was transparently trying to evoke some sort of bluff congratulatory reassurance. She might have more consciously said, 'Tell me, it is OK. Isn't it?' I didn't give her any such release, I looked at her in a concerned way; she was downright worried, and she went on . . .

'I was that scared when he brought the stuff home, I'll be honest with you. His dad's inside – he'll be out soon – but it's not been easy, I'll tell you. Two kids. And Greg has had one or two brushes with the law and the nipper . . . I don't know. So I took Greg to task about it – what with me old man coming back soon and all. But he swore blind he'd found them right and proper – though he wouldn't tell me anything at first, he was upset being suspected. Later on he marched down the police station like and banged the lot on the counter. Bet not many people do that, do they? He's a good boy and that court said it was right. All but praised him.'

She looked proud for a moment, but I said nothing and her expression began to disintegrate. Tears started to trickle down her face. 'Oh where is he, that boy!' She looked at the clock and then out of the window. 'That little bugger's out there, he's round the side of next door's hedge. Last time he did that was when the CID came one day. They didn't pin anything on him then but I wasn't sure myself whether it was a case of "give a dog a bad name" or "there's no smoke without fire". Come on, you know something about those coins, you tell me. You just here to buy them or what?'

She'd changed from snivelling and dallying to being on the warpath and full of latent action. It wasn't a good moment to go into the ins and outs of my being an archaeologist; almost anything I could think of felt too abstruse and arty farty for the context. 'Me,' I said, 'I'm from Cambridge, and I'm interested in the coins and the ring for themselves, but if your son is in any trouble – and you may be right there, a mother often is – then I'm well placed to help him dig himself out. I don't want anything myself and I don't mean him any harm, I want what's right for the objects.'

She didn't stay to hear me to the end and, indeed, went off talking to herself. 'I knew that little bugger wasn't telling the truth.' The door sounded as though it was flung open in a very majestic way and Mrs Philby bellowed for all to hear. 'Greg! I can see you! Get in here this instant! And make sharp about it!'

I could almost feel Greg slinking up the garden path with reluctant but impelled footsteps. It would have made very credible radio drama. Then I heard him hasten over the threshold, obviously the locus for many a thick ear down the years. And then, a second's thought later, he was entering the room I was in. My God he was a big boy; I wouldn't have liked to be on the wrong side of him. But before he could size me up – or, more likely, before I could let myself down – Mrs Philby followed on, looking uncompromising. She took off her apron; I suspected this to be a storm signal, if ever there was one.

Greg went for the lesser of two evils. 'What can I do for you, then, Mister?'

'Never you mind, Greg,' responded his mother. 'I've got a bone to pick with you first. You listen here.'

Me, I sat on the side of the armchair looking stony-faced.

'I want the truth about them coins 'n that' – she continued, pointing to the table – 'and I don't want any of your nonsense. I know about the house with the Indian stuff in it; you needn't think you fooled me.'

My expression remained unchanged but I was stunned; she'd put the two things together intentionally, but for a different reason, in a way that left me agog. As is often the case, a thing which, in prospect, seems the irresolvable crux of an issue, disappears, as in a dream.

'Well if you know they come from there, you know, don't you. They weren't doing no one any good and I thought they might do us some.' He wasn't as happy as he might have been, more cowed and sullen.

'Your father, Greg,' his mother said.

'My father!' Greg responded. 'Don't know what he'd think of you fingering me.'

I thought it was about time I came in, and I did so pretty cutely. 'I'm not from the police, Greg, but they'll be involved just as sure as eggs are eggs if you don't let me help you.'

He looked at me as though I was a social worker he had temporary need of.

'You see, Greg,' I continued, 'when these coins and the ring were held pending the treasure trove inquest they'll have been photographed. And the jury's decision having gone the way it did – and it was technically questionable, I assure you – those photographs will be gone over. You might have been fine if it had been anything else but those coins there' – it was my turn to point – 'they are completely unmistakeable and the ring too. Frankly, you're going to be in trouble – big trouble – for having lied at the inquest, and I think you know yourself that it won't stop there. We don't want to bother your mother with the ins and outs, but you know that, don't you?' I said.

I may have been bullshitting but I'd hit the mark, he certainly did know. To drive the message home I added, 'I saw a couple of uniformed police up there just now, poking around, not likely to be a coincidence.'

He blanched. 'What d'ye reckon then?' Only the vestiges of toughness now.

'Well,' I answered, 'as I was explaining to your mother, my concern is that these things end up all together in a museum rather than being split up, sold, or melted down. I've taken photographs myself in case that happened.'

Greg looked at his mother; she merely nodded, parentally.

'But I've a guess those photographs won't be so very important now,' I went on. 'I reckon the smartest thing you could do with that stuff there is to put it in a museum; it's the nearest thing you can do to putting it back. If they've got it, the heat'll be off.'

Greg grunted, he saw the point. 'I don't suppose there'll be any money in it?'

'Greg!' his mother said sternly.

'What exactly were you thinking of?' I enquired with a benignness that was shadowed by instant removal.

He mentioned a few things for his family that were homely, innocent, low-key. It's funny how I warmed to him and his mother, n'er-do-wells who were also full of simple goodness. The fact of the matter was that he wasn't all in the wrong; there's grey, and there's shades of grey. The irony was that if the objects were in a tomb then they were definitely not treasure trove – since there was no intent to recover. It was a clearer context than the one he'd fabricated. He'd committed a crime getting into the tomb through the house but that was something else – and if he'd gone in from the cliff way there'd very likely have been no crime. In any case, if he'd found the stuff in a context where it *was* treasure trove, then he'd have been the recipient of a fairly large cash award. One aspect of laws is that they get you; another is that they protect you. The lot of the two in front of me was to keep pulling the short straw.

'I see your point, Mrs Philby,' I said, 'but when all's said and done, Greg is doing the right thing and the nation's heritage will have benefitted. What we're talking about is putting it all to rights – as far as this stuff goes,' and I pointed again – 'and I'm sure he deserves a little something.'

I don't know, I left that house that afternoon as happy as Larry, smug, self-congratulatory, contented – I run out of adjectives. It goes to show something. Fate had put the whole lot in my lap, for the immediate taking – I can't claim the credit; it happened. But did I pick it up? No, nothing so direct, nothing so simple. I joined a game part way through, being played according to a language and rules I didn't understand, and I left it thinking it was going to continue as I solely intended. I didn't have the money and I didn't want to be seen to be involved, so, I was going to prime someone I half knew in the County Museum, and the Philbys were going to respond to an invitation, give a good story, and not come away entirely empty-handed. There!

There I was, under the illusion of having solved one problem, triumphantly squaring up to the next. I told James what had happened – I went straight there – and I suppose I was if anything too self-deprecatingly modest. But the tomb was the matter that had to be addressed, I'd had a great shot in the arm, and it showed in my confident ability to get matters sorted. There was no doubt how the tomb was going to be dealt with. My (nameless) conniving with the Philbys meant that the idea of alerting the police and of having to bring the house into things simply disappeared off the agenda. Not that I'd managed to think my way through to doing this plausibly - or managed to think of a way of keeping James out of it. Of course, the urgency was still there and, let's face it, the interest, the thrill, the scoop.

The way in was through the tunnel from the cliff and I wanted to get going as fast as possible. Even in the short time there'd been, I'd got things pretty well planned out in my mind. James would have broken into the tomb - he and his friends had, after all, almost done so, unwittingly, a couple of years back - and it was the school holidays. The aim was to have him discovering the tomb, but more legitimately, though I then realized it would be better if he discovered it already broken into, since that would account for someone having been in there. Either way, it was quite reasonable that he'd come belting across to Cambridge - since he knew me over the Cliffsend site - and we could take it from there. The existence of an entrance from the house was still a problem - as was tying the 'hoard' back to the 'tomb finds' without incriminating Greg Philby; but I was sufficiently buoyant to feel matters would be resolved, and at least James and I were off the hook with certainty. My thoughts had actually travelled on to the problem of properly investigating what was there - and one of the things uppermost in my mind was such damage as had been caused. It was an unknown, a potentially heartbreaking unknown.

James and I, of course, discussed this through in a brief and conspiratorial manner - much inspired by what had happened with the coins. As far as anyone we knew was to know, we were going down to the Cliffsend site by night, so as not to attract any interest but also to clear up any outstanding possibilities. James' parents didn't quibble for long, in fact I don't think they quibbled at all; they'd read the local, and the idea of convertible loot (rather than old rubbish) didn't leave much need for persuasion. I did make a short suitable statement about how worried I was that there might be further ransacking, how we had to go there to ensure that everything was recovered under scientific circumstances. Somehow, the more sincere a subject in its proper context, the more transparent it feels in a lie.

XIII

I went back to my father's house, partly to make some explanation of what James and I were (supposedly) doing, and partly to say that I'd be staying on a bit in consequence. Visits were usually brief, an extension unheard of, and it was the last bit that caught his attention.

'I thought you came down here a bit sharp. What have you done in Cambridge?'

It wasn't actually true that all was peace and light in Cambridge, but that was beside the point. 'Nothing,' I responded. 'As I was saying, I want to do some work at that site at Cliffsend with James, the boy who was here this morning.'

My father looked at me noncommittally.

I was at the midpoint between assuming normal rules of relationship and being in exasperated defeat, so I spelt things out a bit. It was to no avail, but I felt I had tried.

'You won't find anything there,' he said, sarcastically and a little pityingly. 'Someone's beaten you to it. All you got was broken old bits of pottery. Ha! I'll put some tea on.'

It really wasn't worth responding.

'What about that job you've got in Cambridge?' he shouted from the kitchen. 'Haven't you got to be there tomorrow?'

I said I'd phone in and that I was owed some time. There was no point going on about how it wasn't that sort of job, or that my 'work' was a bit larger. No point at all. Just no point. Keep it simple.

'Of course,' I said, going into the kitchen, 'we'll be going out at night. Don't want to attract too much attention after the last time.' We were on the verge of one of those insuperable problems about mealtimes but luckily he was still in scoffing mode. All he said on the practical side was that my sheets were in the washing basket and it was a 'good thing he hadn't got round to doing them'. I felt unhappily certain on the subject of daytime harrying but, well, you can't win them all.

James turned up promptly later on. I'd managed to have a snooze – though I did get woken out of it – and I had also managed to take some essentials from the garage unobserved. The task of putting together foodstuffs was more hovered over, but this too was achieved. I said goodbye to my father and met James the other side of the door.

I felt it was certain that we were going to be stymied by some fishermen being right opposite the 'gun emplacement' – but this wasn't the case – and there was no one on the cliff-top. First we took what little we had up the steps, keeping it close to our bodies, then I drove the car off a bit, while James went inside. I sauntered back, quickly passed the stuff in, and then followed in myself. I'd only reached the pebbles when there was an enormous commotion in the dark back of the cave, and out flew a pigeon. It really rattled us, and I very much hoped there wasn't another biding its time, but in a way it got the fright over with, broke the ice, or whatever.

'Is that a gas lamp you brought?' James asked.

'No,' I said, 'it's a Tilly, it runs on paraffin like a Primus but it does have a light like a gas light. I'll show you when we get up there; I've only got one mantle and there's no glass to protect it. It was all I could get.'

'The tools you've brought mean business,' he said.

'We're going through that wall tonight, that's what we're doing, and that's all we're doing – except having a look round and maybe taking a few general photos. At least we've got kit for that; I don't know exactly what we'll need after and we'll have to get it tomorrow anyway.'

We got everything up the hole and I set to with the lamp while James shone a torch on it. Getting the silk mantle on was the devil, but I don't know when it wasn't, and then I clamped the meths-soaked wick round the base of the vapouriser and lit it. The blue light was like a joke, and James switched off his torch to laugh, but as it dimmed and guttered I pumped up the lamp and turned the knob which released the pressurised paraffin up the vapouriser tube. The light given out was shockingly brilliant in the context, but quaintly yellowish and with its own hiss and fuggy smell.

James was torn between the lamp – which astonished him – and the short tunnel which it lit up so brightly. I was looking along the tunnel at the wall and – not for the first time – I was having qualms about what we intended to do. But then across this was running the thought that I hadn't been happy about that wall the first time I'd seen it. I touched James on the shoulder to keep him from making a shadow, and I went forward with the lamp so that we could both have a closer look. The bricks were old, they were softer and that bit smaller than modern ones, but they didn't look Roman and while the bonding was mortar rather than cement, I wasn't somehow very happy with that either.

'I'm not keen on this wall, James,' I said. 'There's something I don't like about it, but here goes. We'll take out the bricks in this bottom right corner, where you lot burrowed under. You hold the light, here,' I demonstrated, 'I'll have a go first.'

It was actually as easily said as done, in fact it was laughably easy. All I had to do was to loosen the lowest brick by whacking a bolster chisel into the surrounding mortar and then to lever it into the hollow beneath using the spade – the other bricks followed suit. It was quick and systematic and I was able to take the bricks out entire, making a small stack of them, mounding up the loose mortar alongside, sweeping it with my hand. The miracle of it was that the plaster on the inside of the hole I was making remained intact. I was able to free it underneath, chisel through up the sides, and then snap it off by pushing at the bottom so that it fell back onto the angled spade and pickaxe. It didn't work perfectly – it broke – but it was better than smashing through, and more in my nature of doing things.

The plaster taken out was patterned exclusively with dull blue-black mussel shells and was experienced as a foretaste of mysteries. Somehow, also, the removal of the plaster – the making of the hole – had made a connection in more than a literal sense; one could feel there being something on the other side. The moment had come; James was going to be vindicated; I was about to see something astonishing for the first time, aware that I would have quickly to come to terms with how to deal with it. The moment beckoned; it also daunted.

I took the lamp from James and pushed it ahead of me. The brightness was blinding close to, and it was only when I was in and holding the light aloft that I could gradually see, though not to the edges. It was a chamber – just as James had described – but it wasn't vast and soaring in architectural terms, more carved into the oppressing massive – which, indeed, it was. It was strange, quiet, secretive and dead with its arched ceiling and with its overpowering, bizarre shell patterns as dense and convoluted as the tattoos of the Maori. The altar was there, such as it was, and the niches James had spoken of, and the passage leading out on the other side – but that was it. The impression I had was of emptiness; it was like a cellar that had been cleared out.

I hadn't moved from a spot that I'd seen was safe, but being aware of James having followed me made me conscious of the floor and what was on it.

'Stay put,' I said, 'we don't want to disturb anything.'

'What do you think?' he asked. Perhaps he had expected more audible and visible signs of astonishment on my part.

'I think it's strange,' was all I answered. It was how I felt but, anyway, I suspect that fitting words are often fitted later.

I pumped the Tilly to restored brightness and then held it out, silently looking at one segment of the floor at a time. There were things on it OK, archaeological things – most conspicuously bones and pieces of pottery – but it was truly odd how the objects looked as though they had been scattered on swept lino – they even had shadows. I wondered, if I simply wasn't used to what I was seeing; maybe I parochially only knew about the mud-with-bits-poking-out type of archaeology; perhaps – I don't know, Etruscan tombs and pyramids were different.

It was easier to think of practical matters, it often is. What was there had evidently been disturbed – mostly by Greg Philby, partly by James; it had been scattered and damaged (to an unknown extent); some, of course, was missing; while other objects may have been brought in. The fact that these just consisted of bits spread across a bare floor made recording a doddle and I was, at least, pleased about that.

'Easy,' I said.

'You say it's "strange" and you say it's "easy", Jonathan.'

He obviously thought such a discovery merited more. Me, I was thinking on.

'It's great,' I replied reflectively, 'but let's go one step at a time – and the only other step for today is to take some quick photos. Pass the two cameras in with the flash; leave the case outside.'

But that wasn't it. You see, in order to resolve something, to sort it out in my own mind, it has to be approached systematically and it has to fit into a larger picture. James wouldn't have understood. I was, indeed, boggled by what I would increasingly see as the trappings of a rich burial of the Roman period – the bits of pottery were better described as broken pots, including amphorae; the bones were evidently human and in reasonable condition; and I could even make out pieces of corroded iron and other metal, which had thrilling potential. It was all scattered and disturbed, but truly remarkable for all that – particularly if the coins and the ring were taken into account. I, of all people, could see this. It wasn't that the next step to be taken was preoccupying me – which it might have been – for that was as clear as it was simple. No, it was that I had a gut feeling that there was something fundamentally wrong in what I saw, an instinctively felt flaw; it nagged me and I couldn't leave it.

Of course, I wasn't sure and I had literally to tread carefully, while – in some ways equally literally – leaving James in the dark. The first thing I looked at was the room side of the blocking to the passage we had come from. James had been completely right about this, you simply could not see where the passage was from the inside (apart from the hole we'd made) – the plaster was continuous across, as was the pattern of shells. The other thing I wanted to see – in spite of the feeling that I shouldn't – was the entrance from the house end, and so I very carefully picked my way across the floor and then up the tunnel. The tunnel was of the same dimensions and build as that from the shore, with identical tool marks – and this, of course, was interesting. What I particularly wanted to know, however, I partly found out as soon as I encountered rubble on the way up to the top, for the bricks were comparatively modern – they had dents in the top – and they were stuck together with plain, ordinary cement. But then, one of the larger lumps of blocking I found further up had the plaster on it with several layers of wallpaper adhering. At the top, a wall of the bricks survived to chest height, the broken-through hole above being snugly blocked by the back of the bookcase I'd heard of. At the junction of the two there was linoleum – not vinyl – on comparatively fresh floorboards, which were nailed with round nails to a joist of similar vintage. The wall itself had been built within the frame for a door, which reached down to the bottom of the passage; the pins for pin hinges still survived, the wood was dark, dry and shrunken, and the nail-heads were square and irregular.

I was in a little reverie; it was perplexing, there were loose ends, there was disappointment – but I'd escaped the pitfall that the obvious presented and there was something to go on. I hailed James across the chamber, the relief I felt mixed with an indecision about how best to present the news. I stopped my careful progress in the chamber centre and held the lamp aloft. The problem solved itself.

'Do you see those white things making the rays near the centre of the wall patterns?' I asked this and then went and lit both his and my steps to a point of closer inspection.

'They're clay pipe stems!' James said. He was incredulous. 'What the hell's going on?'

XIV

We sat in the tunnel on the other side of the blocking and worked it through on paper, as I said we would. The sandwiches were merely something we didn't want to have to take back, but the coffee was welcome (if instant). Though I had things fairly connected in my mind, writing it out was as testing a discipline as ever and there was inevitable redrafting. There was also much conversation, for not only did I want to carry James with me and to mitigate disappointment, but I also respected his native sense and I wanted to use him as a sounding board. Anyway, devoid of the means by which we got there, and much tidied, we ended up with something like the following:

1. Where the tunnel originally came from on the landward side was not clear since the present house, while incorporating it, appeared to be much more recent (see below).
2. There were different scenarios regarding the order in which the two parts of the tunnel and the 'tomb' had been built, and of the timespan involved. The whole lot could have been quarried out in one go; the middle part of a tunnel from inland to the sea may have been expanded; or a tomb entered from either the land or the shore could have been extended. The last seemed least likely but the evidence on which to make a hard choice was wanting.
3. Whatever, the next event was that the exit from the 'tomb' to the shore was blocked by a wall put across made of arguably post-Roman and certainly premodern bricks. There was access from the sea to the back of this blocking because the mortar was pointed, but it meant the tomb could thereafter only be entered from the land side.

4. The tomb was subsequently plastered and decorated and, by its nature, this all had to be done at the same time. The act had hidden the blocked exit from the inside. Pipe stems used in the decoration gave a crude date for it of between the seventeenth and nineteenth century.
5. There was then a period of time – which may have been of great duration and complexity – when the 'tomb' was accessible for use from where the deserted house now stood. The only certainty about this was that Roman material was taken in; goodness knows what went on in there and it's also, of course, conceivable that other things in general may have been taken in and taken out again.
6. The door at the landward end of the tunnel may have belonged to part or all of its existence. However, the doorway was blocked up – from the outside – in pre-vinyl but otherwise modern times, and a floor was put in externally at about half the height of the tunnel. We knew the blocking above floor level to have been plastered and then to have been wall-papered over several years. All this supposes the house to have then existed. At least latterly the blocked up entrance was behind a bookcase.
7. The most recent event from the house end was that the blocking had been broken through and Greg and James had been in. The former had taken plenty, may have caused the disturbance seen in the process, and had also taken in at least cigarettes and matches. Each of them had put the bookcase back in place.
8. After the sea side of the 'tomb' had been blocked off, what went on in there was for a while a separate issue. At the turn of the century, however, the cave at the entrance to that part of the tunnel was blocked totally by the 'gun emplacement'.
9. Time had given access into the cave again and also to the tunnel up to where it had been blocked off.
10. James and his friends had tried to get through, unaware of what was on the other side; James and I

had, of course, just succeeded with great purposefulness.

During the writing out, James had come up with the main issue several times, and with the fact being taken as increasingly obvious. Never mind the minutiae; never mind the irrelevant; the essential point was that the objects no more made the 'tomb' Roman than they would have this effect on anything else they were put in – be it a museum or a cardboard box.

James took it well – or maybe I successfully led him into taking it well. 'What's your guess then?' he inquired. 'What's it all about?'

Aside from the formality of facts, relationships and deductions, any archaeologist worth his salt always has a best guess of how things might fit together. 'I'd say,' I started, 'that what we're sitting in is no more exciting and no less exciting than a smugglers' passage to bring contraband from the shore unnoticed. I know they exist and smuggling was almost an everyday occurrence this close to France in the eighteenth century. That's probably about the age of it. *Now* the car's on a road outside the cave entrance, but *then* the nearest access to the sea was a mile to the east at Ramsgate and a mile or more to the west at Cliffsend. And it was out of sight of both – a perfect spot. As for the top, what's there? – pre-war and post-war houses. At the time this was built it would have been equidistant from the villages of Chilton, St Lawrence, and Ramsgate – right in the middle of nowhere.

'Makes you think, doesn't it?' I continued. 'A dark night; men in a dinghy; a flashing lantern in the cave mouth down below; the wines and spirits would have been hauled up at the end, as these tools were, and rolled and carried past where our legs are. That place the other side of the wall was probably stacked up with goodies awaiting the equally perilous process of distribution inland. What fear, everydayness, and bravado there must have been for knots of men in there when things were happening, what boredom, anticipation, and hectic action. It may not have been the Romans but it was all here and we're very close to it. After all,' I said, 'the chalk pit known as "smuggler's leap" is only three miles away.'

'The caravan site?' James interjected.

'That's it,' I continued. 'The smuggler was called Gilpin I think, maybe Jack Gilpin. When he was chased he headed his horse for the pit and – at the moment the exciseman caught up – they both, seemingly, went over. But only the body of the exciseman and his horse were found, Gilpin being both folk hero and in league with the devil.'

'I knew about that,' James said, 'now you mention it. He's still meant to appear, isn't he?'

I merely made a gesture and looked up and down the tunnel.

James laughed, then came back to me. 'But look, what about all the fancy shell decoration and the Roman stuff? Where does that fit into what you're saying?'

'The point is that it doesn't,' I responded. 'The only connection would be if the decoration was used to conceal and sanitize the scene of illicit activity – which it would also have put a stop to – but the juxtaposition of the two things may have just been opportunisitic. My guess is that what we've got there is some sort of shell grotto belonging to the late eighteenth/early nineteenth century. It would have been the product of one of the local gentry (as the smuggling may have been) – and inland from west to east, to my knowledge, there was the Nethercourt Estate, the Southwood Estate, and the Ellington Estate. You get shell grottos, and they're a not too easy to explain element of intellectualization and fancy among the gentry of the time, blended out of the "grand tour", neo-classicism, new familiarity with China and India, romanticism, and the Gothic obsession.'

James looked at me quizzically; I responded.

'These were the people with parklands studded with statues and Graeco-Roman temples; they even had artificial lakes with miniature galleys and they employed people to act as ornamental hermits or Arcadian shepherdesses. They had secret societies full of mysticism, devil worship, and libertine behaviour. Sticking shells from the beach on the walls of a pre-existing cellar would be about par for the course for Ramsgate in such times.'

I hesitated, I felt I'd rather unnecessarily put the whole thing down a bit. 'But it's very impressive, and a great discovery,' I continued; 'goodness knows what was got up to in there. And the Roman stuff – which is very important in its own right – fits in. In a way it's not out of place for it to be there at all. I, of course, have no idea where it came from originally but, given that they had it, that decorated room was just the sort of place they'd put it. Indeed the inspiration for decorating it may have been the objects.'

James gave me a wicked look, paused and asked, 'You're sure that stuff in there's Roman?' He was joking, but it was a good point.

'Sure,' I answered, 'as sure as I can be. What's more,' I added, 'the sameness of quality, the condition, the constancy of date, and the type of objects all make me think that it is a grave group . . .'

'And the bones?' James interrupted.

I nodded, 'And if that's what it was, then it was a pretty rich one – richer than any I can think of in this country – and it's a very, very important find.'

That plumped him up – visibly. 'So, what are we going to do?' That's what he wanted to know. 'Tell someone? Excavate it?'

'Neither – well not exactly,' I answered promptly and with a smile. 'I don't think we have to tell anyone, do you? After all, the objects were blocked off half a century ago from a house which is now deserted – our consciences should be clear on the matter of ownership. Plus, the "tomb" was discoverable from the shore; the objects don't belong in there – so we don't have to say where they're from; and, quite honestly, we are rescuing them.'

James didn't need any convincing. 'We're going to do it? The two of us? How?'

'*How* couldn't be simpler,' I answered. 'Since none of the objects are in their original position there's no harm in us simply gathering them up. We'll do it carefully and methodically, of course, but that's what it will amount to.'

'Great! Really?' James was brimming with enthusiasm.

'You tell me if I'm wrong,' I said. 'What's more, it's not going to take any time – we'll do it tomorrow night, easy. I'm sure.' There was much grinning; I was pretty thrilled too. 'Come on, let's go,' I added.

As we gathered the tools James started to panic that someone would come while we were away. 'I'll stay here,' he said. 'Leave what's left of the sandwiches.'

I reassured him – 'Don't think of it; it'll be OK; you need to be fresh tomorrow night.' But I felt what he meant, and the more for him having said it. I remembered not being able to completely get the most perfect of fossils out of the cliffs when I was a kid and being fearful that someone else would find it and finish the job before I could get back. I also remembered breaking that fossil in intemperate haste. 'Come on,' I said, though with reluctance.

And then as I handed the lamp down to James in the cave, the tools having gone, he said, 'Does this mean we're going to forget about the smugglers' tunnel, and the store?' He suddenly felt for the loss of a part of the richness which had been found and mapped.

'I don't know,' I said truthfully. 'We're in a position where we can only get something by not attempting to have everything. It's a bit like life,' I quipped, but James didn't understand. 'Maybe time will reveal a way – the position won't be changed by us taking the first step we're going to, will it?' I dropped through the hole, stood beside him momentarily, and said, 'We're not going to forget it, are we?'

The pigeon that had come in took the opportunity to fly out again. There was a world out there and there was now a dull brightness coming in from it. I took the lamp and turned it off by releasing the pressure with a hiss. My word, I suddenly felt haggard – and James was done in. It was bloody cold too.

PART THREE

XV

I had mixed feelings about James being in Cambridge. He thought it was 'great' – to use his own word – and, at a very simple level, he was doing what he wanted to do. I'm not speaking here of the discovery of new vistas of wonder and opportunity, of beckoning fields beyond doors made manifest. No, I'm talking more at the level of an 'activity' or 'adventure holiday'. It could have been horses, or fossils, or – I don't know – yachting, but this particular youth – for whatever reason interests, and particular interests, are inculcated – was mad keen on archaeology. And he washed and glued, sieved and picked out things with tweezers, put objects in bags with labels and made lists, mounted photographs and plotted on plans. Now I write that I realize that the analogy with 'activity holidays' is not entirely true, for such are created labours of satisfaction with little purpose beyond their pursuit. What James was up to was important, it had to be done and – as I could only really supervise – it was he who was doing it.

I think it was this difference that triggered the conversion of a somewhat detached growing semi-awareness within me into a feeling of alarmed panic. James was a natural at what he was involved in, the skills and understanding came readily to him and he was as happy as a sandboy. So what was my problem? The fact is that it came to me in a nightmare when, as is often the case, I was left with a residual sense of horror – and what might be called the 'punchline'. For all that he had come on, for all that he was enjoying himself, an essential part of the analogy with the 'adventure holiday' remained – for he could still go back. That was it, that was what my mixed feelings were about. He was approaching an awesome watershed about which I suddenly felt terrible responsibility, like death in the heart, and of which he was blissfully unaware – but he could still go back. Should I blow the whistle? Could I? Did I want to? Was it my business? Did I actually have a right to? Life occasionally dumps one in a godlike position where one flounders in indecision or is paralysed in inactivity, aware of consequences but able to do nothing except watch events take their course, and to feel while doing so. Perhaps there are Gods after all; perhaps that is the position they find themselves in.

This business of the watershed was not a matter I'd thought overmuch about in connection with myself, not in anything like such a concrete form anyway. Indeed I wasn't thinking of me at the time but you sometimes see what is important for yourself, if only as retrospection, in the circumstances of others. The thing is that in coming from the background I did – and Ramsgate is only a metaphor for that – there is a point beyond which one cannot just come back from the adventure. But this is too simple a way of putting it; the trap one enters is infinitely more exquisite than a mere one-way door. And I could sense the elements of the diabolical machinery slowly and quietly forming and taking their position about the unsuspecting victim here. He would make himself forever an outsider to the land of his birth and, in return, never become more than a would-be immigrant pursuing a mirage by way of destination.

It sounds so little, doesn't it? A nothing worth mentioning, a mere sentence in passing. But it would rack and squeeze him, buffet and frustrate; it would appear in small things and large, anticipated and unexpected; it would be there to the end of his days. An internal engine of little-ease, never-ending discomfort in the self.

This was all boiling inside me and I did and said nothing.

At a mundane level, matters had gone very smoothly indeed; it was all action, success – and delight. The latter, for me, partly emanated from the almost naughty and uncluttered excitement of it all. The fun I was experiencing was very much at the level of the fun that James was experiencing. I had got back to that. Getting the contents out of the supposed tomb had been a breeze, as anticipated. First, we laid a line on the floor, took a right-angle offset from this, and developed a grid of numbered metre squares. Then we photographed each square in plan, bagged or boxed the objects and subsequently swept up any detritus in each case and put it into a labelled sack. Finally, we plotted the ground plan of the 'tomb' relative to the grid, cleared all evidences of our having been there, and left. It wasn't perfect – here I go again – but it was adequate for the circumstances.

There was a real sense of 'mission accomplished' on heading for Cambridge later in the day. What we'd got had remained locked in the car boot and simply hadn't been spoken of. My father didn't show any interest; what could have hurt me in other circumstances, or that which I would have denied, was turned to useful account. He was in a huff; he knew that (whatever I'd been doing) I would have (and had) wasted my time; and, when I went, he was watching a technicolour war film which he'd switched on part way through and might not watch the end of. As for James, he was bubbling over with enthusiasm and importance when I picked him up. He'd told his parents that I'd asked him to go to Cambridge for what remained of his holidays to help me out. Strange – it struck me as strange – how he could be oblivious to his parents' reaction – as oblivious as they were to how he felt. None of the bonhomie could disguise for me their inner disaffection – which was not because they had, or thought they had, anything to be worried about – but which was borne of a sullen mix of disinterest and responsibility; a suspicious combination of parochial ignorance and being under an obligation to have superior knowledge. His mother had packed him a bag and vaguely mentioned 'his keep'; in another disconnected portion of conversation his father had hinted about him 'making his fortune'. James made an exit fit for a return as the conquering hero. There was much waving.

I might have felt funny going back home with a sudden, adolescent house guest. But I didn't. I'd phoned, I'd explained, and it wasn't a problem. Nor was it a problem about work because I'd simply taken a week's holiday owing to me and after that I knew James would be able to get on on his own at home during the day. It was all pretty jolly.

Everything had to be done at home, it had to be done on the QT, and was all the more fun for that. One end of the living-room and half of the kitchen were requisitioned for the purpose and looked the part in no time. As for a blow-by-blow account of the practicalities – I think we can happily dispense with that. Enough has been hinted of the industry and processes involved and I think, after what I have said, that sufficient can be read into the situation regarding James.

One thing that one would wish said – for once and for all – was that every bit of gridding and separate bagging, and of the painstaking identification of objects on photographs and their plotting was a complete and utter waste of time – from an archaeological perspective – except to prove a point. It seemed clear – and the more one thought about it the more obvious it was – that the objects simply didn't belong where they were found. Other than this, the impression was of the fragments having been promiscuously scattered and nothing much – let alone anything of interest – could be said of how they had been secondarily positioned. True, there were seeming centres to the distribution of some things – particularly glass and uncremated human bone – where there were crumbs and small fragments, but the most likely explanation for these was that pieces had been trodden on. On the whole, the material had every appearance of having been quite literally kicked around – most of the fractures were modern.

The fact of the matter is that we really might as well have simply gone and picked the objects up in the first place without bothering to do any recording at all. And the point having been demonstrated, that was how the whole lot was then treated, as though it had just come jumbled in a trunk from an unknown origin. This was a great release from inhibitions and unnecessary time-wasting niceties; it permitted us to look at what was important here without deflection – and what was important was simply the assemblage of artefacts and their inferred original context.

I am aware that I have thus far been coy about stating what exactly there was, perhaps annoyingly so. I can only explain that I have been consciously presenting the story I tell as though it were unravelling afresh. The plain fact is that, though we'd seen bits of things in the tomb, and though we'd seen scatters on plan, a clear picture only really started to emerge when the sorted fragments were spread on the living-room table and the glue had been got out. Even then, of course, it was a gradual revelation, and a while before we were sitting back looking at everything laid out in, at least, a tidied up and semi-reconstructed state.

The silver coins and the ring removed by Greg Philby were certainly near the top end of the 'treasure' spectrum but – while the most obvious – they weren't on their own. What he'd missed was a load of scrap gold and silver – I say load, maybe (to be frivolous) a wastepaper basket full – and what this consisted of was pieces of gold and silver embossed plates and vessels, roughly cut up, folded, stamped flat. The silver was darkest blue-black, dirty (in contrast to the coins), while the gold was bright and could easily have been mistaken for new brass – indeed, it took time for us to talk of it as 'gold' rather than 'gold-like'. Gold and silver the pile might have been, but it was in bad shape and, in a way, unimpressive. I was frustrated that there wasn't another coin – not for want of looking, or hoping – it would have been so handy.

What else was there? Well, the bulk of the pottery pieces – thick, coarse, and buff-orange – belonged to two great amphorae which, when reconstructed, leaned, slender on their pointed bases, nearly four feet tall. And then there was other pottery, of which there was masses, consisting of fine, red slipped, relief-figured sherds which – put back together – made a small suite of luxuriant Samian ware. Glass was also present – I have mentioned it – and this had, of course, suffered greatly and was by its nature difficult to sort and reconstruct. This is to generalize, however, for the pieces of one particular item were as distinctive and easy to deal with as the amphorae fragments among the pottery. The object to which I refer was a bellied jar of thick, plain blue-green glass, unornamented except for horizontal lines, with arched handles on its shoulder, and with a knobbed lid which fitted within its everted rim. It was plain, but massive and stunning. Other than that, there was a whole series of delicate little flasks and beakers and bottles which, with our capabilities, we could only reconstruct in part. Some of these items showed signs of heat; indeed there were lumps of the set remains of melted glass.

Then there was metalwork, which again sadly showed much evidence of recent senseless damage, but some of which had evidently originally been in contact with great heat. There were the circular discs, about two to two and a half inches across; three were at least recognizable as such at the time, though there were a lot of other fragments. What can I say; they were black, wafer-thin and fragile, they had embossed designs and one of the complete ones, I remember, was a lion's head, face on. Then there was a whole run of bronze buckle fittings and mounts, including a virtual entanglement of perforated strip which was bent double along its length. There were a lot of pieces of iron too – though reduced to rust, most being fragmentary and broken. There was nothing we could do with this without expert conservation sighted by X-radiography. But any fool could see there were bits of a shield boss and of a sword – as well as some pieces that were evidently different.

The coins and the ring were a great clue; the scrap precious metal, pottery and glass added detail of a unique collection; the other metalwork, in some ways still enigmatic, was to be the complete giveaway. Many will have recognized the objects I speak of, but among the cognoscenti there will, I'm sure, be one or two who would like to ask me about the human bones. Well, they were there; I borrowed an articulated skeleton and laid it out at home on a board on the floor; then we built up the skeleton from the 'tomb' next to it piece by piece. There was nothing unusual – except, that is, that there was no cranium or lower jaw.

XVI

So much for what there was – that is, what there was in a way. It, I hope, sounds exciting – it still is, no doubt – but I also hope that you can imagine that special excitement that we, the discoverers, had. It has to be said that it was frustrating to have been able to have gone only a certain way with the type of objects I have described and then to have had to stop. There were skills, facilities, and input of manpower required that we knew were beyond our limits. But we felt pretty good about being responsible and, if full reconstruction, restoration, conservation and even the identification of some things remained to be done, well, we had had both the kill and the lions' share and we had been able to do our best by something we considered 'ours'.

And what was it all? It was then, it was increasingly revealed to be, and it has never yet been surpassed as the richest Roman grave group ever found in the British Isles. It was simply glorious, a great discovery, and we felt it. But that is not to say that there is no difference between then and now, other than a heightening perception of worth, scale, or rarity. No – and this does not diminish what has been said – that was the point in time at which things both seemed to become clear and at which suspicions were raised that they weren't as clear as they seemed.

At first sight the obvious and clinching thing about it being a grave group was the presence of human bones. After all, wasn't it one of these that James had taken away in order to originally prove to me that he had found a tomb? And indeed, conversely, what more fitting place for human bones to be found than amongst a grave group? But there were a number of things which struck us as odd and raised doubts slowly – as they are raised slowly in situations where there is no reason to think anything is other than it looks. I can't remember where it started but I can remember the feeling being vague, peripheral, inconclusive. There were other more live or positive facets of what was happening to which our attention gave a natural priority.

To start with – though I'm not putting these in any order – there was the fact that the bones could be seen on close inspection to have been gnawed in places by large rodents – that is, rats. This could easily occur if a body were left exposed prior to burial and this in turn could have given some explanation of the head being missing – for I checked that it hadn't been hacked off – but the presence of all the small bones really went against the idea. And then, what were all the small bones doing there anyway? The material we were dealing with had come from somewhere else and it was only in the comparatively recent past that one can imagine people being overmuch bothered about collecting the bones and, even if they were, then it takes a lot of determination and expertise to effect such a complete recovery. We, it must be remembered, had swept up all the loose soil, sieved it, and picked among the residue.

A second train of mildly disconcerting thought started with the large blue-green bellied glass jar which I have described, for what it looked like when it was reconstructed was no more and no less than a cinerary urn – though it's always possible such containers had other uses. But then there had been fire around, as evidenced by all the bits of affected glass and metal which have been mentioned. And then the sieve residues produced what hadn't been obvious on site – because of the white chalk floor and dust – fragments of calcined, that is cremated, bone. Though it could well have proved to be animal bone.

In a way it was all something and nothing. If one likens archaeological evidence to the pieces of a puzzle then – apart from the fact that the greater part is going to be missing – it is a common finding that there is either no solution which will account for everything, or that there are several. There wasn't anything here that was outside the sphere of the usual sort of residual perplexity, and one must remember that we were only part way through. Burial archaeology is full of much more bizarre conundra – like seemingly articulated skeletons with bones upside down, or apparent men with the remains of a foetus in their pelvic cavity. The cremated bone picked out piece by piece amounted to quite a pile – probably little less than would have filled the jar, allowing for how it must have been ground up. And though the cremated bone may have been animal I must say I had my doubts. Teeth are the most resistant under such treatment and there were fragments that looked human – though they could have been pig. I thought it was something that a specialist would sort out and, to tell the truth, what the teeth in the cremation made me wonder was where the skull had got to.

I should mention that the cremated bone was 'it' from the sieve residue. Everything else merely consisted of the smaller fragments of the objects for which larger pieces had been recovered by hand; as is the way, only some were of any use. There was nothing else that was coeval with the Roman grave group and what is perhaps more remarkable is that there was nothing else, full stop – that is, unless you want to count entirely modern cigarette ends, spent matches and sweet wrappers. This was incredible when the date and probable usages of the supposed tomb were considered; it must have been positively scoured before the Roman remains were put in there and there was no evidence at all – and I was expecting evidence – of people having been in and out up to the time it was closed off from the house.

However, we had other things to think of. We did, after all, have on our hands a treasure of sorts which we had come by, if not illegitimately – or downright illegally – then in what can only be most politely described as an unorthodox fashion. And it was our fervent desire that it received all the attention it merited – in terms of further restoration, academic study, and public attention. But how was this to come about? We couldn't exactly just pop up with it without explanation for where it came from. The analogy got closer – as analogies sometimes do – it was like having committed a successful robbery and then having the problem of legitimizing, or laundering, the proceeds.

James thought we might 'discover' it all at Cliffsend, where the site was that he'd found, and where Greg Philby had said the coins and ring came from. The last circumstance, of course, made the suggestion very tempting for it would have neatly reunited all of the material. It was a good idea, but I didn't like it. One reason was the practical difficulty of faking a findspot; though Greg seemed to have got away with that in a big way, and there was the option of pretending that the material had come from there at some time in the past – we even thought of enlisting Greg's help with this. James was disappointed, particularly as we got quite carried away when it came to the thought of involving Greg, but the greater reason for not following the seeming heaven-sent route was that it involved inventing a context for the objects. To not exactly tell the truth in pursuit of a justifying end is one thing, but to attach spurious facts to archaeological remains would have been inexcusable wickedness.

That, of course, was exactly what Greg had done; he had made a unique hoard come into existence – when it wasn't a hoard – in a place where it had never been, and this would appear as the truth in every relevant book for all time, and goodness knows what would be made of it. The thought of this made me hot under the collar – we had to do something about it, not make matters worse or add another lie to an existing one. Certainly, the material we had in our hands was without a context – apart from, fortuitously, being together, and having been found in east Kent – and it should stay like that. But how was the 'legitimization' to occur?

This problem had been in the back of my mind from when the decision was taken to empty the 'tomb' and I had had a rather vague but I thought sufficient plan. Now it seemed full of holes and prone to any number of things going wrong. The trouble was that neither of us could think of anything better. The idea was that I'd put the material into auction in Ramsgate and buy it back, but some of it was so huge, while other bits were very delicate – and much of it was stuck together (and so well) with modern glue. Besides, James was too young to either place a lot or to bid while I could hardly appear in both guises. And though it was a desirable part of the scheme that the laundering would only cost the auctioneer's cut of the proceeds, what was I going to do with a cheque made out in a false name I'd given? That aside, the thought came up that there was always my father; he might moan, he might deride, but he might well do the buying and, after all, no one would know him from Adam.

James was going back – to school – and the stuff had to be packed. The two did seem to go together; it was departures, ends of chapters, whatever. We decided the most practicable and neutral packaging was spirit boxes from outside off-licenses, since these are rigid with an interior space that can be divided in different ways by using the separators that come with them. Identifying labels were taken off using lighter fuel and 'stamp lifter' – a liquid with which philatelists will be familiar. The amphorae were a problem in their own right but here we thought it best to have no packing at all and just to send them as they were. Some delicate objects we couldn't bear to pack up, particularly smaller glass items, but we reckoned this wouldn't matter because no one would be counting – especially as it was part of the plan to add what was being put in on the day of the sale as a 'late' lot.

There wasn't a sale that coincided with James going back; there wasn't one for a week or two. I checked that on the telephone and it meant a second trip; but it also meant not hurrying at something. Although the boxes, thus, weren't going immediately, they made a mournful pile.

Everything done, James and I metaphorically just sat and looked at one another; in actuality we fidgeted in nervous activity and found communication difficult. It was like it is when someone has to go and the point has been reached when all is packed and ready, what is appropriate has been said, and the fact of the parting has been acknowledged, accepted, internalized. The time of departure of the train, boat, plane or, I dare say, spacecraft, is known and is awaited in an awkward limbo; how awkward will come to mind if I merely mention unscheduled delays. The ways, mentally, have already departed; as a phenomenon it is scarcely less stressful than to find of a sudden that someone has gone without saying goodbye. I had anticipated it, I had planned that James' last evening in Cambridge would be something of a culmination. In my imagination we would have been able to talk of this and that, and of his time over there – the sort of rounding and encapsulating of an experience. But it hadn't worked like that.

Partly this was because of the way such situations are and one element of this is that goodbyes do not stand alone but of themselves imply travel and destinations, however manifested. For myself, when I thought about it, I quite nakedly wanted somehow to have done with it all and to get back to my normal work, the pressing requirements of which were taking over my thoughts. As for James, he had already made the transition in his mind. His thoughts were in his carryall, with his jar of 'Cambridge' marmalade; a 'Cambridge' coffee mug; and a 'Cambridge University' T-shirt. Although the exact nature of what we had been doing was a confidence (that I was sure would be kept), James was already regaling his parents and schoolfriends – Brian, Paul, Peter, even Greg! – with some version of his experiences. And one thing I was positive of was that he was seeing the land I was in – a few feet from him – from that other shore. I laughed at myself for my concern that he wouldn't be able to get back; I mean, I actually laughed aloud.

And before James had had a chance to come out of his reverie and respond to this my thoughts went on. I realized starkly (again) how very little I had in common with James. He came from the same place and he had the same interests I'd had when I was his age. But even if, through some science-fiction time warp he were exactly me, then what of it? The only connection was the site at Cliffsend, the coins, and the 'tomb', and – insofar as that was all sewn up – that was it. There was no more, no reason why there should have been any more; he would, I thought, make an acceptable employee on one of my sites, maybe, but I was disinclined to mention it.

'You know,' I said, 'if you were to get the train – now the stuff doesn't have to be taken – you could be back this evening.' He didn't demur.

XVII

It is difficult to retell things as they were revealed exactly and with authenticity; the perceptive reader may have got there before me, but it only tumbled to me about the skeleton on the way back from the station.

I pulled in to the kerb – outside a takeaway in Cherry Hinton Road – and I thought it through. It was simple and obvious. If all the bones of the skeleton were there – and we had sieved out fragments of the smallest – then it was inconceivable that the bones had been found somewhere else and had been brought into the 'tomb' along with the rest of the material. The reason for this has already been stated in passing – no one in even the fairly recent past would have had the desire or technical ability to achieve that. So it was inconfutably the case that not merely the skeleton but the whole body had been put in there. It was, after all, a tomb! Ha! But, all the same, nothing had changed regarding the Roman objects; they still didn't belong there – originally, anyway. And while the introduction of the objects and of the body may have been broadly contemporary in terms of the 'tomb's' use, the skeleton was as much of a damned nuisance in my eyes as the 'tomb' itself had been. Here we had a premier Roman grave group, neatly separated out from the bogus context it was found in, and – guess what – it then turned out to be contaminated with a post-mediaeval skeleton, and I had the sneaking suspicion that that may not have been all.

I tend to set about resolving things in what I call 'watertight compartments' – I sort out one area of a problem before I go on to tackle what is logically the next. Here, what I thought was settled – indeed, literally packaged up – was all up in the air again. At least, that's how it seemed to me, for I was tired and fed up – 'it was all I needed' – and rationality and sense of proportion were not close to hand. I was actually in a bad temper over it in no time.

When I got home I was less pleasant than I might have been, and I made a beeline for the box of human bones, setting its contents out on the table, which I cleared in a peremptory way. The bones didn't help me, they didn't add to what I knew, and all that looking at them did was to increase my frustration. I looked at the other boxes and thought of going through their entire contents again, searching now for contaminating material that might be the same age as the skeleton. I felt I couldn't face it. I argued with myself that if there'd been anything that was post-mediaeval rather than Roman I'd have surely seen it – for, after all, there always had been the possibility of material of later dates being there. Whatever, I unpacked every sodding box and went through it grudgingly, doggedly. There was nothing. I even got and tipped out what we'd picked from the sieve residue: I went through it with swimming eyes – but there was nothing there either. As it happens, I came to the photomontage – the pasted together photos of the tomb floor – last: it revealed in irritating detail what I had already worked out. With the help of a magnifying glass I could now go over what we'd realized was a focal point for the scattered human bones. Kicked around and trodden upon they may have been but, if you believed in it, you could see the odd vertebra, some ribs, the knee caps, and some foot bones all in their relative positions. I took a felt-tip highlighter to the photograph, even adding a sketched outline. Turning the screw on myself.

It was at this point that some fairly caustic domestic comment came down the stairs. I was in no mood. The last thing I'd thought of – because of the outline – was where the skull had got to, and this became an obsession as of the moment. There was no reason to it, it was just an available avenue of activity. I had the strongest suspicion as to where it had gone – Greg had taken it, whole, there were no pieces – and I reckoned I needed to see him anyway to check up on the coins.

I know, of course, that I followed in James' tracks and caught the last train to London – driving was out of the question. I also know that hanging around Victoria for the 'paper train' – something I hadn't done for fifteen or twenty years – was like a nightmare sandwiched between two bouts of fitful sleep. And I knew that my arrival at Ramsgate station coincided with when I would normally be waking. But, as when one goes to sleep and later wakes, there truly seemed to have been no passing of conscious time; no opportunity to prepare myself. Usually I at least arrived in Ramsgate with some head of steam but there I was, tired, confused, and stripped of the comfortable (if not totally effective) defences I had devised over the years; the place had the better of me from the start. As I made my way up the long flight of steps from the platform underpass to the early morning emptiness beyond, the only confidence I had was that my day was going to be awful.

Once outside, I did have to decide exactly what I was going to do. It was chill, it was early, and my stuffing and drive had gone. Going back seemed as good an option as any but I did a deal with myself; I would not see my father or see James, I would talk to Greg Philby and then I would go – go home. That was, at least, a plan and, aware that I had to waste two hours before I could reasonably call on Greg, I dawdled off in the direction of his house.

The two hours went in an appropriate way. First, I was stopped by a police constable suspicious of my look and the bag I carried at such an early hour. I turned my bag out with pathetic readiness to demonstrate the innocence of its contents and volunteered that I was going to my father's, giving the address. But I felt degraded by the experience, being taken for something less than I was and having to defend and justify when I was used to going unimpeded about my everyday business. And then, second, I went into a rather seedy café – it constituted the only choice there was – because I had to eat and drink something and also because I needed to use the lavatory. It was doubtless mostly the mood I was in but I felt self-consciously out of place and commented on, while, at the same time, I found the food, the decor, the noise, the smells – and just everything – as a foretaste of a minor circle of hell.

I was at a pretty low ebb all ways round when I reached Greg Philby's and looked at the house from the pavement. Nothing much had changed. Although I wanted to get it over with, the house also beckoned to me in my current condition: I rather fancied sitting on some washing with a cup of tea and sympathizing with Mrs Philby. And she answered the door, but any lifting of my spirits was short-lived.

'Bert!' she shouted, looking back towards the kitchen. 'It's that archiwatsit back.'

'You leave him to me,' I heard. Mrs Philby disappeared, replaced by a hulking man in shirt sleeves. 'My boy came by those coins and things legitimate, see, a court of law said as they was 'is. Now you listen here, he's sold 'em as 'e 'ad every right to do. By law! It ain't none of your business poking your nose in. You can consider yourself lucky as how I'm in a good mood. Now fuck off, and don't come back, see.'

I realised straight away that it was Greg's father, back from having repaid his debt to society, but I didn't feel like arguing, either to the closed door or after having knocked again. I looked at the door for a minute or two and then went out into the street (behind the hedge) to reconsider my position. I sort of stood, or squatted, or crouched, or leant, for a while saying 'the coins, the coins' over to myself and feeling that, in some bizarre way, my sudden interest in the skull was to blame.

While I was there, in a shocked and useless state, Mrs Philby came out of where her gate might have been and, holding a shopping bag, walked to where I was as though I wasn't there.

'I don't know why I'm telling you this Mr Riley but the coins went to that man in George Street. And that's it.' She went to walk on, turned and said, 'And don't come back or tell anyone I told you.'

I thanked her, I had enough sense to see that she was helping me as best she could. Then on the spur of the moment I asked, 'Where's the skull?'

'Oh I made him put that in the dustbin, horrid thing.'

'Which dustbin, when, where?' I queried.

'The one at the house; there! It hasn't been emptied. You don't want it do you?'

I nodded. She was incredulous, but she also sensed that she could give me something and she went back to return looking no different. Then she pulled a plastic carrier bag (which had contained sports shoes) from out of her shopping bag, handed it to me, said 'Merry Christmas', and walked away.

It was a skull, but though it was what had brought me where I was, it was no longer of principal interest; I didn't bother to get it out of the bag. Of all the naive fools! I'd had the coins, the ring, actually in my grasp, and I'd just been too clever. But the ring, the ring – I chased after Mrs Philby; she'd disappeared, but then I saw her through the window of one of a complex of shops; a small self-service food shop. It felt downright strange going in and walking up to her as she browsed, her thoughts in another dimension to mine; it was as if I was going to proposition her in some unwelcome way, as indeed I was.

'The skull,' I opened, 'the skull is fantastic.' I said this quietly, as can be imagined, but that in itself made the situation seem more embarrassing. 'The coins, I'm upset about them, but I'm grateful to you and I'll go now, and who knows? But the ring, that was yours, is that down in George Street?'

She replied though, really, she wanted me to go away. 'No, I thought of selling it before Bert got out but the jeweller I took it to said it wasn't worth nothing, wasn't hallmarked. You see, it didn't fit me,' she explained, 'far too big. Well then you come and I supposed it was going up to that museum but when the coins didn't I thought I'd just keep it. Greg did give it to me after all.'

But it was the way she looked at me that told me the truth. She had the ring there, in the coin bit of her purse, in the middle section. She'd known that her son had got the things in an irregular way and she'd wanted him to give them over. When the father had turned matters round she'd hung on to the ring because that was in her power, and it wasn't the ring as such, but what remained of the ability to undo the situation her son had got himself into.

'You know,' I said, 'If you let me have the ring I promise you it will go into the right place. I'll give you some money for it as well, willingly.'

She looked at me. 'What I want to know Mr Riley is if you have this ring if you'll forget where Greg really got the coins from. 'Cos I think you're the only one that knows, aren't you? I don't want no money; but no stirring things up, right?'

I promised, and I took the ring. I said I'd hand it over to a museum.

King Street, when I got there, rather unshaven, was less than helpful. He was evasive. 'Nah. I ain't got any Roman silver coins at all. Them you turned down went, but there's a few other brass ones in the window.'

I felt I couldn't mention Greg, or be too specific – though, of course, the coroner's court decision had been public enough. 'Look,' I said, 'I heard a rumour about these coins. You've got your ear to the ground, I know: I'd be interested.'

He looked at me as though he had no idea what I was talking about.

I was out of my depth, but I wasn't giving up. 'Look, I'll buy at least one, several of them from you for a very good price – get you some of your outlay back.' I flushed.

He folded his tabloid back to the racing page and took a biro off his desk, testing it in the margin.

'And I'd try to get a decent price for the others if you give me a day or two.'

He spoke, 'Only a London dealer'd be able to cover that sort of thing and the goods wouldn't stay round here for long.' He jerked his lizard-like neck to one side, then the other, coughed, reached for a cigarette and lit it.

I felt sick, powerless, dishevelled; I didn't need to ask any more. My interest in the coins was a subject of non-interest because he'd sold them and he couldn't sell them twice. Moreover, I knew I would never get anything out of him since he would have sold the coins for a lot more than he would be telling Greg, and he wouldn't be telling the tax man. No, the coins had disappeared and that was that. As for King Street, he took an imaginary piece of tobacco from his lips and examined it; they were filter-tip cigarettes.

XVIII

I sort of kept my promise to myself and went to the railway station directly after King Street. I was down, of course I was down, and the fact that the coins had gone was constantly replaying in my mind – each time, afresh, striking me as both incredible and a total certainty. All the same, I could feel the ring – I'd put it in the ticket pocket of my jacket – and I surreptitiously took it out and looked at it as I walked along, as I sat on the bus, and as I waited on the station platform. It was something, certainly that – and I had it.

Sleep came, though the first I knew of it was being woken by a ticket collector when, as it proved, the train was nearing London. I didn't know quite where I was: the carriage had been virtually empty and now there were more, and different, people in it. I felt as degenerate as unshaven men who sleep across tables in railway compartments are taken to be. Maybe the other passengers thought I was the worse for drink, or a down-and-out. At least one was decent enough to remind me about my carrier bag when we all stood, waiting to get off; I couldn't tell you whether it was a man or woman, young or old.

As things would have it, I had a little time to wait for a train at Liverpool Street. My impetus was broken by external circumstances, I had slept a bit, and I began thinking about feeling a little more human again. The food was takeaway – from one of the outlets there are in big stations – and it was eaten standing up, but, while not making me feel settled, it did make a difference. I also managed to buy a disposable toothbrush and to have a wash; a shave seemed to be out of the question and a shower in one of those places was beyond what I'd have felt comfortable with. I went to buy a newspaper but came away with a copy of *Exchange and Mart*; my eyes hadn't scanned those columns for donkey's years and the whim took me.

My train was in, it was a compartment carriage, and I sat reading on my own for quite a while. It didn't fuss me when – shortly before the train was to leave – I was joined by two rather noisy and, well, common girls; that's how life is. They chattered on sixteen to the dozen and I occasionally looked up between gobbets of browsing. In many ways it was as if I wasn't there, though they shared a few nudges and comments about me. I don't know what age they were, I suppose that sort of age when those not inclined that way look rather too old to be at school. Maybe they were older than that, maybe. Both had black hair and were probably pretty, though it is difficult to tell sometimes when girls wear the more strange types of teenage garb. There was no ignoring their presence, they were full of *joie de vivre* of their own sort, smoked, listened to headphones – one each, from the same machine, while talking – and seemed to have to run and giggle while going up to the lavatory and back.

As I said, I kept looking up and while I might have considered them annoying, I actually found them refreshing. They were enjoying life at an enviably simple level. If I was looking at them rather much, they didn't appear to notice it. One got out at Bishops Stortford and the other, keeping the earphones, propped herself against the corridor side of the compartment, put her legs up on the seat and closed her eyes. For me, my thoughts moved from her having a simple enjoyment of life to her simply being a female creature. The ear I could see looked so tender, the lobe with its pendant earring and the white skin behind it. Her hair was tousled, and in the position she was in she appeared warm and relaxed with an association of comfort, home and bed. Her face was pretty, and I went over each feature, thinking how lovely it was and how the different elements related one to the other. I tried to imagine her unkind, unloving, unreasonable, indifferent, vicious – and I succeeded – but that wasn't how she looked then. I'm afraid I did also rather linger over the shape of her, the lines and contours of her body, imagining what I couldn't see, taking her, in this way, from the clothes she was within. The train started to stop, she opened her eyes, gave me the sweetest smile imaginable, said goodbye, and got out; it was Audley End.

Audley End, next stop Cambridge, that brought me back to where I was. When James had left there'd been the problem of somehow bringing the Roman grave group we'd got out in the open. When I left it was because the human bones had unexpectedly turned out to be nothing to do with the issue in hand – a red herring I promptly followed. When I got to Ramsgate it was to find the 'hoard' that it had all started with had largely disappeared; the arrangements I had felt secure in left aside, disregarded. I was at least returning with the ring

– which I had supposed was safe anyway – and with the skull – which I rather wished I had left on the train in London. In many ways I was back where I'd started: I had to do something with the bones, then I had to do something with the objects. 'Not all bad,' I thought, fingering the ring as the train rattled on; 'and I did get a photo of the coins, which I can now use.' It was coming together in my mind again, but there was still the problem of tying the contents of the suppposed tomb and of the supposed hoard . . .

'But first,' I continued in my thinking, 'first something must be done with this fellow.' And I took the skull out of the bag for the first time, putting it carelessly upside down in my lap as my hand went back to fish out the lower mandible. While in this action – and I will never forget it – something about that upturned skull caught my eye. It was the back teeth – the back teeth had dental fillings in them! It would take an archaeologist, so inured to the remains of long-gone mortality, to miss the bleeding obvious. Post-mediaeval be damned – the body was modern! I felt nauseous and unclean. The lower jaw was the same; I pushed them both back, got up and went to wash my hands, taking the bag with me. In the lavatory, on the floor, was the partner of the earring I had seen in the girl's ear, a piece of brash glitter. I put it in my pocket with the ring, for no reason.

It wasn't an easy day, my word it wasn't. Things had gone from bad to worse at home, but that seemed incidental, something that had to be borne. What was I going to do? There, as I'd left them set out on the table, were the bones of an unknown person, though now with a skull – and very different for it. The reason why the contents of the 'tomb' had been in there was a mystery enough originally; I had skipped over the implications when the body was just post-mediaeval, because it was merely a nuisance, but now that it was relatively modern – well, it's facile to say that it had become rather prominent in my thinking. The body was sufficiently recent and the 'tomb' had been blocked off sufficiently long ago to conclude that there was every likelihood that the two events were connected. It was all a little exotic, it had happened a while back, but what had happened was that a body had been concealed in a cellar. It was chastening that the facts hadn't changed from when James and I sat in there and simply decided that all the material was Roman and didn't belong. Now there was a murder. Our view had not been wrong, but blinkered.

Murder! That was a new one for me, I'd never thought of skeletons in that connection before. I looked at the bones but there were no obvious signs of violent death; not that there need be, of course. There wasn't an implement and, come to that, there had been nothing, no trace of clothes, not so much as a fly button – we had swept up everything and sieved it. It was strange, I wondered what the police would make of it, and their involvement in itself was fast firming up as an inevitability. There didn't seem to be any way of getting round it. But what were the ramifications? The whole story was going to come out of the 'tomb', of James and I breaking into it and taking everything from it; of James having broken into the house (and me knowing); and Greg having not only broken in but having stolen things and then having brazenly lied in a coroner's court. The latter was something James and I had both known about from the very beginning and, of all ironies, I'd promised Greg's mother amnesty for her son, on that very day, while getting the skull.

The whole edifice, the story, had been built as necessary in order to save and preserve an important Roman grave group. It was a good thing to do and there around me were the objects, all boxed up. There was no doubt the grave group would now be as secure as we intended it to be – except for the coins having gone – but, other than that, everything now looked shabby and indefensible.

Oh, it was going to be grim! I'm writing when, one way or another, I'm out of it, but to have had the curtains pulled back at the time, to have all the machinations exposed to daylight and the common gaze, to have story and motives gone over by law officer, court and profession, these are, even retrospectively, prospects which induce a cold sweat. Having said that, it will be clear that an exposé didn't occur, but I wasn't to know that, and how this came about (or didn't come about) is an essential element of the story.

At the time, I had no way of knowing how things were going to work out – and I was panic stricken. In the first shock, complete confession seemed to be the only answer. But having acknowledged that – and its consequences – I began to work backwards to the most desirable alternative – that is, the one that salved my conscience while having the fewest undesirable effects. My wildest thought was just to say to hell with the whole lot – bones, Roman things, everything – what did it all matter. The girl in the train wouldn't have been bothered about it. Why look for problems, why not let life simply go on, taking such pleasure as comes one's way. It was a delicious thought, made more delicious by thinking back to the girl, but such an approach to living had always been only a delicious thought to me and nothing more.

There are those who think about doing things and happily never quite get round to it; my curse has been that of being incapable of doing nothing.

Slipping back to the dis-ease of myself, I *did* – seriously – toy with the idea of destroying the evidence, for the murder, on my reckoning, was as cold as could be, the perpetrator, if alive, drawing their pension. I mean, it was only circumstance that I saved the skull from the bin men and I did almost lose it before I realized its significance. But I couldn't quite swallow that option. The thought of putting the bones somewhere else was equally quickly dismissed, out of conscience, for that would be to destroy irrecoverably the connection with the 'tomb' – which was perhaps the most important fact there was about the body. Nor, as I remember, could I take to the idea of keeping the bones in a box and of saying and doing nothing on the basis that no one knew anything before, so there was no loss. No, the way I reckoned it was that the bones had to go back where they came from, but that all the police were going to get was the briefest of phone calls saying that human bones had been found – and where. Given a little bit of on-site reconstruction, I argued, the police would, one way or another, have every bit of evidence there was to do with the body – the Roman objects not being obviously connected – and it was for them to come to conclusions and to pursue matters.

I've no doubt that many will be aghast at my lack of scruples, but it was me who was in the predicament. I was, actually, pretty unhappy about it at the time. I mean, the notion that the police would have all the evidence was partially untrue, while the idea that we couldn't have been of very great assistance was a polite fiction. What I'd decided at the time I am writing about now is that the bones were to be put back. Doing this would mean the Roman grave goods could then be dealt with as an unaffected and unconnected issue, though how exactly that was to be done remained to be resolved. However, I was taking things one step at a time and what was immediately necessary – and which seemed even crazier then – was to go straight back to Ramsgate, with the bones in the boot of the car.

Days like that are funny timewise. Do you know, it was just mid afternoon and not only had all that has been described happened, but the pace of events was continuing. There was no getting off that particular ride just then. Two calls had to be made.

The incident with the policeman and the bag that morning had given me awkward feelings about my father. I couldn't go down there again and not see him; what I'd done seemed sacrilege, so I rang. The gush of feeling, albeit covered, was, of course, on one side. He was in unenthused 'message received and understood, over and out' mode, and the short conversation, as usual, only left me buoyed up by the impetus of my own input. He did ask me where I was phoning from and whether both of us were coming, but I could always deflect the irritating – almost without conscious effort – at that stage of contact with him.

The other call was to James – who, unavoidably, had to be put in the picture. He was, of course, not back from school, but I was disoriented. And his mother, without thinking any harder than I had done, explained that she 'wasn't at work because of a cold and wasn't that lucky'. She then went on and on, on and on, about what a lovely time he'd had in Cambridge – of course, he'd only got back the evening before but I was so confused and things had moved on so much that this seemed to have very little relevance. However, not to miss an opportunity, I said that he'd left a few things (which he had) and that as I was going to be in Ramsgate I'd drop them off eightish that evening.

XIX

My father was as difficult as could be. Partly this was because it had been such a short time since my last visit, partly because there was too much spontaneity in recent arrangements, but mainly because he'd come by a bit of grit, an opportune seed of aggravation. As he said:

'Police were round here, said they'd seen someone calling himself Jonathan Riley early this morning, wanted to know if you were staying here.' He drew his breath in through his teeth, adding with a nice touch of despair, 'Well, what was I meant to say?'

'The truth,' I countered, sounding flippant. 'Was this before or after I telephoned from Cambridge?'

'Look Mr Clever,' he replied, 'this person not only gave your name as his name to the police but he also gave them my name and address. Perhaps the less I know the better.' He got up, switched the news on, and continued, 'But it's not very nice for someone who's getting on and lives on their own.'

Watching the television was predictably quiet and tense, not helped by the fact that I knew I was going out and wasn't going to say where. I don't think I even got a grunt when I did announce this and left. My humour was a little restored by the time I reached James' house and his parents were good value – little did they know I had a body in the boot! There was a froth of what they would have seen as gentility; even a glass of sherry was proffered (though there was consternation when I said I didn't want it). There was a lot of chat about how James had enjoyed himself, how he was interested in all sorts of fancy things, and how grateful they were to me. There was also a strong undercurrent that he was 'back to school now', and 'had to get back to his studies'. Mr Stone (Ted) clearly couldn't resolve in his own mind the conundrum that James had done some work in Cambridge but that he hadn't been paid anything, as though he'd been on holiday, but then he hadn't paid to be on holiday. He contented himself by casually but authoritatively establishing a few points – as befitted his position – the thrust of which, of course, was to expose archaeology for what it was jobwise – a non-starter.

To James I seemed to be a bit of an intruder. After all, he'd only said goodbye to me the same time the previous evening and there I was, breaking into his reassimilation. I had to get him away; I had to get him away and talk to him. When I did there was a slight distance and a feeling that things had gone bad and had gone on without him (which they had) – I cursed myself for leaving the ring in Cambridge – but this was, of course, all submerged by the news of the body. He was shaken, and the more so when I drew his attention to the cardboard box in the back of the car and then opened it.

'What are we going to do?' he asked. Neither of us had bargained for this.

'We're going to put him back,' I said. 'I've thought about it and it's the only way.' I explained further, I felt I should do, but James didn't have any difficulty with what was being proposed and for all I could see that this was naive, it comforted me. He didn't have a problem either about going down with me – or, indeed, in offering to be the one to telephone the police afterwards. But, at the same time, I felt that even he wasn't sure how interested and involved he was. And I suppose I felt the same way; it was a bit like being presented with a rejigging of the day before's roast. I certainly remember how lacklustre the actual going down to the tomb was, as was the prospect of going back into it. Body in a box or not it was all rather matter of fact with neither of us being at all worried or scared; it may have all been somewhat odd but what there was was familiar to us.

That mood lasted until we got into the tunnel, having hauled ourselves – and the box – through the cave roof. There was a dark and rather nasty smell which made it seem different, and it was an uncomfortable age before the lamp lit. Nothing looked changed at first but there was an air of unfamiliarity, and then – horror of horrors – we could see that 'our' hole in the bottom of the wall was choked with rubbish, most prominently beer cans, bottles and plastic bags, piled against it on the 'tomb' side. It made us feel nervous as well as nauseated – there was the presence of other people there – a lacklustre situation suddenly turned charged and tainted.

'We still going in?' James asked flatly.

I was quite incapable of decision. 'I will if you will,' was the best I could manage.

We agreed to leave the bones where they were, ripping the top flaps off the box to use to give ourselves some protection while crawling through into the 'tomb'. That corner of the 'tomb', it turned out, had been used as a midden and as a lavatory – liquid would have run out there. As for the rest of the 'tomb', well it contained squalor to match; the debris of a party is far too effete a way to put it. Furniture of the mattress, rug and armchair sort had been dragged in and had ended up being variously abused, overturned, and set light to. There were broken bottles and cans everywhere; the remains of cigarettes and food; batteries and even syringes, durex and spray cans. The walls had graffiti on them, the shells had been smashed where (presumably) bottles had been hurled at them, and areas were burnt and blackened. To think of the immaculately cleaned and otherwise pristine eighteenth-century whatever that we'd left! It was ghastly, horrible, an outrage. And to think what would have happened to the Roman grave group – and, indeed, to the human bones – if we hadn't taken them out. There was justification here, and those who'd done what we now saw would have done it whether we'd knocked our way in or not, they'd only used our hole in the wall as a lavatory. But the overriding feeling was of how nasty it all was.

'Let's do whatever needs to be done with the bones,' James said. 'And then let's get out of here.'

I was revolted by the mess and repelled and panicked by the feeling of gross intrusion that went with it. At the same time I realized that the furniture had come from the house, and that there was every chance – given the state of things – that the way in had been left unblocked. James didn't want to go, and I could understand this, but I was driven by the opportunity. I'd got little out of James about the house – though I'd tried – and now it was being actively destroyed. I had to go. I promised not to be long, but I had to go, and I left James where he was, with the lamp.

Feeling my way quickly up the tunnel, fully prepared for stumbling here and there, I found the top to be not only open but to have a wooden stepladder propped against it! I climbed up and poked my head into the house. The bookcase that had blocked the hole had been pulled over and the contents were strewn about. It was all silent as the grave and I think such light as there was – enough for me to see it was the inside of a house – came from the street lamps outside. I pulled myself in.

It was eerie, it really was, but I immediately had the strangest feeling I'd been there before. I went around all of the rooms of the downstairs and everything had been turned over and slighted. But the odd thing was that everything was there for this to happen to. In the debris of the kitchen there were bits and pieces – packets, tins, and utensils – of types that I'd not seen since my childhood. And there was: one of those tall cupboards with doors and a flap that comes down; a grey, mottled, stove-enamelled cooker; a white 'Belfast' sink with the tatters of a ridiculous pelmet round it and the support for a wooden drainer; a lino floor – worn through with wear; and painted walls.

The place was like some sort of time capsule that had suffered both through age and through being barbarously ransacked. I couldn't throw off the rather vague feeling of familiarity as I walked about, looking and turning things over. It's peculiar to see the debris of an ordinary home – as it might be where there'd been a war – and to see it frozen in time as, perhaps, with a sunken liner. And for there to be that personal feeling, which I could only put down to the era involved and my long fascination with the place, albeit from the outside.

There was certainly something about the remnants of long faded curtains in the living-room that caught my eye and I tried to imagine pictures where there were just the ghostly indications of frames on the wallpaper. The carpet had gone, but I was taken with the edge of the floor – around where it would have been – being stained brown. No doubt that that was where the carpet and some of the furniture downstairs had come from, and what was left was in a confused mess. But it did include smaller and more personal items. There was some knitting; there was a man's slipper; there were lots and lots of inconsequential things. Most interesting for a moment was part of the crumpled insides of a *Radio Times*: I strained my eyes, holding it close to the window with the most light – 1961 – twenty-five years back. When I thought about it, that fitted fairly well with my consciousness of the house having become more and more conspicuously overgrown and deserted.

I dearly wanted to spend longer – even in the light there was, even if I was feeling spooky – but James was down in the 'tomb'. I toyed with the idea of going down there and trying to get him to come up, but I didn't. But what I was determined to do was to go upstairs. I didn't know why but, equally, it didn't take me long to find the room where all the Indian stuff had been. It was on the first floor overlooking the sea, the vast, rich, red-patterned carpet was still there as, smashed, were some of the larger pictures – prints of scenes. But it was the spectral images made by soot and daylight of weapons that once adorned the walls that was so interesting. There had been spears, there had been swords, there had been shields, rifles and other pieces which had made less identifiable shapes. The one I liked was next to the mantlepiece; there was still the nail there on which an armour piercing dagger had hung.

The furniture in the room, such as was left, was pretty beat-up but, it must be said, there was a sort of oriental flair to it. That is, with the exception of a slope top display cabinet which took my attention. I happened to have known a piece of furniture like it, it was ebony veneer, dated from about 1820, and the glass was spun – the sort that's thinner in some places than others. I say the glass was spun, it was also smashed, and crunched softly underfoot. The display board behind the glass was still there and this very much caught my attention because – in a home-made way – it had been modified to be used for coins. The back was angled, with strips of wood running along and you could see that the coins had rested on these like plates on a dresser; there weren't any coins there, only shadows.

The base board had not originally been meant to be angled, I could see that because there was a gap at the back. I wasn't the first to try to lift it up but I was the first to succeed – the cabinet wasn't locked, the top was just jammed. Of course, broken glass slid into the base of the cabinet but there among the debris was an Indian coin that had dropped down, a square silver one, and I picked it out and pocketed it. There was also, strangely enough, a book – an octavo book with quarter leather binding. I held it to the light at the window: it was titled 'Selections in Prose' and when opened proved to contain blank, lined pages – that is except for the first ten or twenty which were covered with writing made with a dip pen and blue-black ink. Writing I say! It was only the original account of the finding of the grave group that had been in the 'tomb'!

I was so excited; I was just so excited. I wanted to tear off and show James what I'd found – and that brought it home to me just where I was and, so to speak, how out on a limb and vulnerable. It was at this time that I realized that the back board of the case, the other way up, had originally been used to display the grave group. Or, more exactly, the whole case had been, for on standing back I could see that the recessed base below would have held the two amphorae at an angle with the cremation jar in the centre on a pedestal. It was fantastic, absolutely fantastic. I had – by a miracle – the evidence that the

Roman material was a grave group, I could prove it did not consist of disassociated objects; 'hoard' and 'tomb contents' could be shown to be one, and I knew where they came from – just nearby, from a mound. It was incredible, literally incredible, that these things had been found in such a bizarre place and rescued and that details of their context a century and a half or two centuries previous had turned up and was in my hand. On reflection, it isn't that much of a coincidence because the two things are more likely to be found together than apart but, at the time, I was agog. I still am sometimes, reliving it; it's the sort of experience that keeps emotion and importance in spite of time passing – there's a thrill to it yet. And there's a thrill to what happened next.

XX

There was light and noise in the street, not much at first, a car stopping, doors being opened. I'd no sooner seen it, and the men that got out than – to their evident consternation – a regular police car came roaring along, flashing light and siren going. The consternation of those who would capture by stealth was nothing to mine and I ran like hell out of the room – which was a pulsating stroboscopic blue – and I flew down the stairs. By the time I'd reached the ground floor the police were making short work of forcing the front door. I flung myself through the hole to the 'tomb', pulling the ladder askew as I went. Feeling, feeling down, not able to run as I wanted in the dark tunnel, I could hear voices behind and above me. There was a light, a voice which said 'Stay there, sir!' and a tumble as the ladder slipped leaving a policeman enmeshed. This all happened as I turned and hastened on with no seeming interruption in my flight.

The voice had alerted James, who I found standing, the dimming Tilly lamp by him.

'Police, police, quick!' I said just audibly, not mentioning his name and only pointing in the direction of the hole.

He slithered through first; I turned the lamp out and crawled through myself; then I pulled the rubbish behind as best I could. We sat there very quiet, I at least consciously controlling my breathing and with my temples throbbing. I knew the mixture of relief and continued fear that animals must experience as they wait for time to tell whether they have or have not eluded the snapping jaws of their predator.

We had got where we were with little to spare; the police were in the tomb and, seemingly, all over it in what felt to be an instant.

'Where is he?' was simultaneous with a more authoritative 'Come out now, sir. We know you're here and it will save us all a lot of time.'

There was quiet – spent by us in frozen fear – and by them – it would seem – in flashing their torches around. The message was to be repeated, but by then they could see there was no one around and betweentimes were simply boggled with where they found themselves.

'What a fucking queer place – is it a mausoleum or something?'

'Bloody hell, it's weird. I've seen nothing like it. It's like satanic rites.'

'Just dropouts, drugs – look at this fucking mess – and don't touch that syringe. We'd better get it properly reported, no doubt sealed up.'

'You lot with the bloody siren, we'd have had him, now we've got more work to do.' Evidently the boys in blue had followed down.

'Where'd he go?' one of them asked, heedless.

'Must've given them the slip back there, doubled back into the corridor I wouldn't wonder. Not here is he?' This, it was becoming clear, was the voice of the principal one of the CID. 'Anyway, you lot get up there and search the house; Oh Jesus, don't say you didn't leave anyone on the doors!'

They went. It was quiet. We waited for what seemed a while –and we were in the dark. James pulled at my jacket and, in response, I crept slowly along the tunnel after him. It was all perfectly silent until we got to the base of the makeshift ladder – when we knew the sand and pebbles would make a noise.

Knowing that, I whispered, 'The bones.'

'I thought you wanted to leave them here?' he replied.

'But, not . . .' I started.

'You go back for them if you want Jonathan, but give me a chance to get away, right.'

This brought it home to me that we were still in a trap; the police might be outside the blocked cave and, anyway, there was only one way up in the car.

'James, you won't believe the book I've got. I've got it here. It was upstairs. It's all about the excavation of the original burial. It's an antiquaries . . .'

James was creeping away, oblivious, towards the slit of darkness amidst the blackness. I went after him. There were no police outside.

'Let's go along the shore,' James said.

'Look, the car's there; if they're going to put two and two together they'll do it anyway.'

'*I'll* go along the shore then,' James replied and he slipped off, keeping close under the cliff.

There was I, conscious of being covered with chalk and all sorts of other crap, feeling and, no doubt, looking as guilty as hell, and my only way out was to drive into the middle of it all. At least I was giving James cover – they'd only seen me. I gave a thought to the bones, but not a second thought, after all the boxful would have made a very suspicious thing to be found with. I opted for boldness, knowing I would crumble if stopped; anyway, I'd never have got up the 'Chine' without my lights on and it could only be done in low gear. But, much as I felt there was, there was no one watching me. Indeed, when I got up to the top, such people as I could see – and I didn't get too close – were looking at the house and had their backs to me. I drove away unseen, even permitting myself a small laugh of relief.

I couldn't wait to get into my father's house and he was asleep or, at least, in bed. I went up and closed the door of the room I had, stretching out the moment by switching on the bedside light, before the pleasure of devouring the book which was my prize. I ran my hands over it, closed, in thrilled anticipation. It was in rather good condition: quarter black leather, minimal gold tooling, raised bars across the spine, with 'Selections in Prose' blocked on a piece of applied red leather; it was about a foot by nine inches (I never could fathom the different octavos), the end boards were faded green textured cloth, while the pages were rubbed at the edge. The end papers were marbled, then there was a title with what the book had been intended for – 'Selections in Prose' – then there was a hand-drawn title on what had been the first of the plain, lined pages 'Antiquarian Notes on East Kent, J Skelton, 1862'. A miraculous exactitude in the writing, an almost inconceivable regularity.

And then there was it – for there was only one 'note', for whatever reason: 'Discoveries in an Ancient Tumulus at Pegwell near Ramsgate, Kent'. I have actually handled a few diaries, notebooks and manuscripts of antiquaries in my time and, looked at from that point of view, what I had was fairly ordinary – indeed, in some respects, it was relatively inferior. But such comparisons were not of moment. It wasn't a site notebook, it wasn't a diary, it was the manuscript for an article – for all articles of such date would have been submitted in handwriting to be set up in print – and it certainly read like such an article. I actually wondered whether it had been published in *Archaeologia Cantiana*, so finished and rounded was it, and the possibility remained with me until I was later able to check and to draw a blank with all possible journals of the time.

Most will have guessed long ago that what I am writing about is the grave of Clodius Albinus. Some, indeed, will have guessed the likely content merely on sight of my name, for the windfall discovery gave me at least passing notoriety where all my previous assiduous delvings had given me none. But for me, then, with the book in my hand, it had all still to fall into place in the reading. The funny thing was that it was all set where I'd grown up: the burial, the discovery and excavation, the hiding of the objects with the second corpse (lest I forget) and, of course, the rediscovery of which I had been a part.

But I am getting ahead of myself here for it was me who came up with the idea that the burial was that of Clodius Albinus. This put the discovery in the superleague of interest and importance. No anonymous burial this, however rich; no, this was *Britannia's* own contender for the reins of the Empire. Doubtless his corner of the known world must have backed him in his brief appearance as Emperor; doubtless it must have felt his loss and death when he and Septimius Severus clashed in Gaul. His followers would have got back if they could and may reasonably have brought his body for befitting burial in a defiant spot overlooking the Channel and the gateway to the province. Though the Severans were to restore order, the burial place would have seen Septimius' body going the other way, for he was the only emperor to die in Britain. Embellishments aside, the identification of the burial with Clodius Albinus caught on and stuck; it's not capable of absolute proof but it's got a high probability. I created in tangible form the famous son no one had ever known they'd even had, but I have always believed it.

The text had no illustrations – they were missing, in a separate folder, if drawn – but they were alluded to. Even in their absence they gave something. Figure 1 was of 'Blewitt's Mill' at Pegwell for, what do you know – the mound the mill had been on was the tumulus! That was really neat and it had only been recognized for what it was when repair work was going on – to cure a tilt. I knew there had been a windmill in Pegwell Village – it's in an early nineteenth-century print I have – but I didn't know its name and it (and its mound) were certainly long gone by my time.

The discovery – brought to light by things appearing in the pub – produced a conflict of interests which was amusing to me then because of its topicality. Skelton, of course, as soon as he heard about the discovery, was hellbent on excavating the tumulus but there was not only a windmill on top of it, but the windmill was being repaired in time for harvest. It would seem from the article that the miller was less understanding of the needs and importance of antiquarian study than Skelton might have hoped, but I saw this as a plea on Skelton's part – a plea archaeologists perennially make – underlining constraints on their work as a hedge against possible criticism. All things considered, Skelton had done rather well for what Figure 2 was of was the pit dug *inside* the windmill. In modern archaeological terms it must have been horrific, but it's a grand thought.

I wouldn't have trusted Figure 3, even if I'd been able to see it, for it purported to show the grave group. I'm afraid that what with labourers digging a hole six feet deep (with pickaxes and shovels) inside a building and what with the techniques of recording there would have been, I wouldn't have given more than decorative value to any careful arrangement in an engraving. To be fair, I suppose it would have shown in some way what Skelton thought had been found, but it would never have been an accurate representation of what had been there and exactly how it was.

When the account got to individual objects, however, it was interesting for it was pretty well a check list of what James and I had actually got – even if the illustrations were, again, missing. While the account wasn't detailed: it proved the various objects to be a grave group; it proved the coins and ring to belong to the same group; and it rather firmed up the existence of a few things of iron which, recognizable then, had suffered by the time we got to them. It also proved that a skeleton was not part of the discovery, only cremated bone.

The cremated bones were said to have filled the glass vessel and the pottery was said to have been in association with it: I can imagine the illustration of the grave group, for this element, looking like washed and neatly stacked crockery. The ring, coins, and scrap were, seemingly, in a group with this lot – and it did strike me that the number of coins was specifically mentioned as thirty-one (though at the time I attached little importance to this). But there were also the remains of a 'great fire' which had objects among its debris, and the debris had had charcoal in it, and it was near this that the amphorae were found broken, the earth 'smelling still of incense'. (I suspected immediately – and still think – the amphorae had been full of resinated wine.) It was in this area that the 'iron frame of a camp stool' was found; without this original identification one would never have known it from the pieces which survived, but it was later reconstructed in a fairly convincing way.

The manuscript had confirmed all sorts of things but it also added two important pieces of information; one was that the burial had been under a tumulus, the other, the mere existence of the camp stool. The grave group – unprecedented for a British discovery – denoted a person of standing. The coins of Clodius Albinus – rare items – mint and struck from the same die, suggested contemporaneity and some possible association with him. The ring, magnificent and made for a cameo which had been removed and then replaced with a gold coin identical to the silver ones but cut to fit; this makeshift was perhaps the greatest clue. But the importance of the tumulus and of the camp stool was that both were emblematic of a person of high military rather than civil rank.

That clinched it for me and I went to sleep that night a discoverer – a person who finds something worthy of headlines and history books. Of course, the finding isn't everything (in a way I hadn't found it), it's the appreciation that it *is* a discovery that counts as much. And I might as well mention here that two of the other pieces of ironwork when subsequently conserved proved to be the dies which the coins had been struck from; the key parts of a travelling mint – together with scrap gold and silver. Their presence – indeed, their abandonment – was a level of proof one could never have anticipated or hoped for.

XXI

Naturally, I have wondered how what I am writing will go down. It is, perhaps, merely a felt obligation discharged and nothing more, and if I die and it comes to naught then what will it matter? When I started writing I thought what I had to say pressingly important; could I have, I would have kept myself alive to do it. Now – and I think partly as a result of having come so far – I feel it is relatively unimportant. It doesn't matter. Damn it, it doesn't matter about dying in the end – whereas one is always believing there must be preciousness in life when in the midst of it – so what's some unimportant background to an unengaging foreground. To say this of one of the greatest discoveries is only to bring perspective. My inclination is not to destroy what is here but, more slightingly, to deliberately leave it unfinished – as I have done all my life with books found disappointing in the reading.

But if it occurs, what will be thought in the reading of this? I suppose – if you are there, reader – I am talking to you! It's strange communication, writing. What would we say to each other if we could? I expect it would be banal, polite, embarrassed. Have you found what I have written in any way exciting, interesting, and compulsive? I, ironically, have found the greatest interest in the incidental detail I have tried to suppress, except as necessary to carry the story, for this has provoked much thought. I suppose we live and then we mull over that living. There is one tangential matter which – reader – I do find of passing fascination, and that is how credible you've found all that you've read. I recognize this as a strange question coming from me – since I am merely relating what happened – but I would be interested in the answer, from a philosophical point of view. I think this is in my mind just now because the present was most in danger of losing credibility with me the morning after I'd fallen asleep in bed with the book taken from the house.

To me, everything that had happened had some reasonableness or connectedness about it – no matter how exciting or extraordinary. But no, I see as I write this that you are not going to see the point or, at least, will find the stress I lay puzzling. The fact is . . . It will be remembered that my father knew nothing of the truth of why I was in Ramsgate, of what I had been doing, of anything I may have intended to do; a false trail had been laid all the while to the site at Cliffsend and I had never made the slightest mention either of the 'tomb' or of the closed up derelict house it was under. Well, he'd already had his breakfast, as usual, and, as usual, was fitfully waiting for me to have mine so he could wash up and go out when he said *a propos* of nothing:

'You know that old house on the West Cliff you've always gone on about? The one that's all boarded up and overgrown?'

This, as can be imagined, stunned me; I was suddenly fearful that the police had started to piece things together.

'Mum, when she was in hospital,' he continued, 'had a bed next to the old girl that owned it. You didn't know that, did you?' He looked at me condescendingly. 'Mum was quite a conversationalist but she didn't let on because the woman was secretive about it – Council would have liked to know – but Mum recognized her, she'd known her after the war, and your mother had a wonderful gift for names and faces. Anyway, the two of them got on well and even corresponded once or twice when Mum came out.'

My mother had known the owner of that house! I suppose that was as incredible as the introduction of the topic itself. No one knew who owned the house, that was the whole point, that was how the place had become so extraordinary. I had to act quickly, though I wasn't sure to what end, for my father, having successfully sprung his bait, was quite likely to go on by failing to remember any more and by making out that he'd thrown the letters away because he 'didn't think I'd be interested'. At the same time, I wasn't in a position to do more than to appear to have a passing or longstanding interest in the topic – certainly not an urgent or current involvement. But he was one step ahead of me.

'I'm going down the town now or I'll miss the bread. Don't suppose you feel like getting a bit of air,' he added, putting his shoes on.

When he was gone I rifled through the locations where I knew odd letters that were kept would be. The position of things doesn't change much in old people's houses and certainly my father hadn't done anything since my mother had gone, other than to throw great wadges of stuff away. Maybe, maybe not: I kept searching. There aren't many letters in such homes, particularly if you screen out official correspondence and known handwriting; anyway people like that tend to throw letters away unless there's a very good reason to keep them. I couldn't help but notice, not for the first time, that missives from me didn't come into the category of being worth retaining. But I did find what I was looking for. There were two letters, in their original envelopes, both very similar, inconsequential, short – but both containing the phrase 'I know you will keep to yourself what we talked about, Mary'. The first was headed 'Sanger Ward', the second 'Dunbarry Nursing Home', both were simply signed 'Margaret'. But I could see the full name at the bottom of one of the letters, as it had been impressed through from the sheet before in the pad – Mrs E A Hooper.

I'm going to stop going on and on here. It's been weighing on me. And I now find myself in a situation where what seems important to me changes, growing and diminishing, looming and fading, with a will of its own. I suppose I must be bewildered – that's one certainty. I feel anxious and fearful, half interested, half trying to control my thoughts and put them elsewhere, but – at the same time – it seems like it's all going on somewhere else and that it has nothing to do with me. Besides, I'm told that 'All this thinking and scribbling isn't doing you any good'! Isn't doing me any bloody good! What *would* do? But here I am again with this rotten invasive incidental detail which is so superfluous – and embarrassing. I should have said all I felt I needed to straight out, and succinctly – and been finished long before. But do you know, now it is scarcely worth giving time to, this very unimportance is a raft to which I can cling in laughing defiance of a tossing sea of the incidental. Discipline, my lad; obey your own orders.

I later went to see the woman – this Mrs E A (Margaret) Hooper – partly, I own, to discover if she was dead, which she wasn't, though she was very old and consciously near to the end of life. One reason I must have gone was out of sheer curiosity about the house, which was much more important to me than my archaeological interests – but the archaeological interests were there, if only as a rationale, and then there were the bones in the cardboard box, left liminally and still in mind. I had no idea how I was going to bring any of these matters up. I only knew that a great opportunity had suddenly been revealed and that I was going after it with the most threadbare of credentials and, intentionally, before there was opportunity to think. That said, one might still ask what impelled me to invade the privacy of a reclusive stranger but there you are, that is one of the mysteries.

In the event it was all no problem at all. My credentials were better than I could have forseen and, indeed, Margaret Hooper seemed under the impression that I was there by invitation. This frail old woman, it turned out, was far more in need of my help than I was of hers, and that was the way it went. She was terrified of the house being damaged and broken into – she had heard of it happening over the years and had been powerless to do anything. For legal and emotional reasons it was impossible for her to sell; long-term financial and health problems had meant she could neither live there nor admit to it being hers. It was a corpse, so loved in life that it could not be buried, but the decaying of which was never from her mind's eye.

I took the decision to be easy on her. I guessed she would never go to the house and I also guessed no one else would make the connection to bring the house to her. I meant in her lifetime, for she was gracefully discarding the flesh, her colour was going and she was becoming ethereal, meeting death half way. The decision proved right, though I am pleased to say that she lived on a while . . .

Enough of that. I didn't tell her the state the house was in in any fullness or exactitude – even her worst imaginings could not have taken her that far and, in any case, what she wanted was the softened truth. I obliged with talk of 'vandals' and the police 'securing the house' and 'keeping a constant look-out'; it's wonderful how words can be used to not convey meaning, especially to a recipient who is a willing party to the deception. But the damage done, to her, was in a way a fear past as in a war which, however dreadful, has been survived so far. It was not that it was unimportant and not that it did not hurt, but that the sum of the suffering was outweighed by the urgently felt need for what had been happening to be brought to a halt, for the nightmare to stop. Her desire was that I look after the house. It may sound surprising, I suppose it did take me aback – though in a welcome way – and I accepted without demur. She, for her part, had it all worked out and I was to be given legal power of attorney; there would be full authority for me and continuing anonymity for her. Although time would reveal strong reasons why I might have taken on such a task I can honestly say that I did so because of the long standing lure of that house, because it was opportune, because it was escapist, and mostly because it just felt right.

I had brought up the subject of the 'tomb' and its discovery, by way of an explanation of how I ever got into the house; I didn't mention James to her – I never did. While she hadn't been in the 'tomb' she knew all about it and, far from being reticent, seemed to want to experience it through what I could tell her. I had to go over the details of the floor, the size, the shape, the decoration, and so on, prompted by queries. The connecting passage with the shore was, of course, news to her and was the only thing about which there was any flicker of unease – possibly because it meant a way into the house from the outside. Apparently she and her husband had called the 'tomb' the 'mausoleum' because there was a skeleton in it, and it was he – she volunteered – who put all the things from the showcase upstairs down there – for a joke, because she didn't like them around, and because he wanted the cabinet. The half of the entrance to the 'tomb' or 'mausoleum' that wasn't blocked off by the flooring that was put in was walled up and plastered over. She told me this, in a very matter-of-fact way; it was all completely innocent. As for the grave goods, she said I was welcome to them!

So, all the problems relating to the grave goods and to the body vanished. I remember the timely arrival of tea and biscuits and my mixed feelings of weakness and euphoria as I sat stilled in the stream of conversation. It meant in the end that I was able to forget about the 'tomb' as far as the grave goods went, simply by reassociating them with the cabinet (and book) – which I said had been vandalized. This is the story there has been previously and it has never given me any qualms; from an archaeological viewpoint it was as good as the truth – indeed, infinitely better than the partial truth might have been. Ah! . . . there's something I've missed out.

Later on, when I'd moved into the house, I found an inventory of the coins which had been in Margaret Hooper's husband's collection; the ring was included and so were, not thirty, but thirty-one silver denarii of Clodius Albinus. So the last of those coins hadn't been lost or mislaid early on but nor had it had been there in the tomb for us to find; my thoughts very quickly turned to Greg Philby. Basically, if I could re-associate a coin that had never been near the treasure trove inquest with the objects from the tomb then it would be as good as a fingerprint to irrefutably tie in the supposed hoard. So, I went after Greg; as I wasn't going to risk the house, I hung around the street and waylaid him. He was OK, what I was talking about was, for him, something in the past to which he was indifferent, but he must have had a good feeling about it and he was friendly. It was, perhaps, for him like meeting one of his former schoolteachers. He came right out with it 'Yup, there was thirty-one. That Brian lost it.'

Brian! I wondered why I'd never got hold of him - but, equally, I'd never had any reason to. However, I had his address and it wasn't long before we were tête-à-tête; luckily I'd had sufficient time to cool down and I played him to the most advantage. He told me what he'd done when 'thick-head Greg' had first shown him the coins - 'I dropped the lot, see, that's what he thought, but I kept one in my hand, and he was so busy fuming and scrabbling around that he never twigged. But,' he admitted, 'he was pretty angry - he's a big bloke - but he'd brought the coins and the ring to me because he didn't know how to market them and he knew I'd dealt with the Cliffsend lot.' There was a nod and a wink here. 'And I drew his fire by saying I'd only take five per cent commission rather than the normal - so that cooled things down. But he didn't really know what he'd got and I, well, I had some checking to do. I took a specimen which Greg let me have down to that dealer in George Street - I'd have brought them to you, honest, but I was suspicious about them having come from the site and I thought you mightn't like that. So, anyway, that's where I hit a problem 'cos old whatsit kept sidetracking and ignoring me till I got angry and said, "Look there's thirty of these" - and, would you believe it, the other bloke in the shop was plain clothes. Oh, I felt that caught; talk about win a few, lose a few. But he was one of the nice sort and I told him they were Greg's and how he'd found them fair and square and he told me about "treasure trove" - silver and gold - said he knew Greg but, if it was all straight, he'd give him a chance to go and hand them in.

'I was stymied,' he continued, 'but the bit of the message that came over to me was that if they were treasure then Greg would get the value - and I'd get a cut. So, I went and told Greg, I was worried - not half as worried as if I'd known then where they had come from - but I put a good side on it, and I think his mum had been on to him; it was a way of getting things legit. But after the experience with the farmer with the other lot of coins it was lucky,' he winked, 'that Greg had found what he'd found on the beach.'

I remember smiling knowingly. I knew, and Brian knew I knew, that even if he was innocent as far as the theft was concerned, he must have lied to the police and coroner. I also sensed that he was still scared of Greg, but I didn't know the extent of this. 'Brian,' I said, 'I hope you can lay hands on that thirty-first coin.'

'I couldn't sell it straight off,' he responded, 'because it suddenly got all very legal, to do with the police, and statements and that. So I put it on one side and acted dumb; lucky I did, I hadn't realized just how identifiable those coins were. Not a lot around, or maybe there are,' he added, parenthetically.

'Lots of them, Brian?' I asked that quickly and with a general air of hidden meaning.

Brian flushed, 'I didn't know,' he said, 'honest. It was after everything I took them down to the bloke in George Street – the thirty coins, that is – and him and me made a deal as to how he was going to sell them in London and give me a cut. But when I went back, he was hopping, he said they were fakes – clever fakes – and though he'd passed them off, it was as such, and he'd got a lot less than I'd expected. I was fixed and the only way to keep Greg away from George Street was to tell him the bloke knew. Funny thing was that what Greg thought he knew was about Greg and that old house – never mind, same difference.'

'I sincerely hope you have that thirty-first coin;' I said this for a second time and, again, firmly. I let him drive a hard bargain, getting a good price for a fake, extorting promises of secrecy. What I did was to simply put the thirty-first coin in with the material donated to the British Museum by Margaret Hooper. A comparator microscope did the rest ... the coin was from the same die as the one in the ring and the thirty that had been photographed. There could be no doubt that they were the other coins and the ring mentioned by Skelton.

When the objects were donated to the British Museum (under my power of attorney) they were rightly hailed a national treasure from the outset. The discovery was big news and then, after expert conservation, there was an exhibition which passed into the not much smaller permanent display that is – I believe – still there.

There were a few residual difficulties which are worth mentioning in the closing. One was Greg Philby for, whatever had happened, I didn't want to drop him in it. However, he was either unaware of the promise I'd given his mother or he didn't trust it, and he asked for the theft of the coins and ring – together with miscellaneous eastern curios – to be taken into consideration when he was arrested on other housebreaking offences. This could have been embarrassing for my suppression of the 'tomb' but – its funny how things work out – he'd never said that was where he got the coins and ring from and Margaret Hooper confirmed that they alone had remained in the house! I told the police that I couldn't say what had been in the house and what had gone missing; I didn't give them any encouragement and they had enough to pin on Greg for other misdemeanours. So, in a strange way, I was able to keep faith with his mother.

What of James, such a main player in the whole thing – he, after all, made the discovery. One could say that once the 'tomb' had no role in the version of the discovery that was put out, then nor did he. But the interpretation, and the implication that I had shoved him out and grabbed all the credit, is simplistic and untrue. No, there could have been continued involvement for him by some manipulation but he vanished away and, at the time it became an issue, recognition was of no interest or relevance to him. All the same, I am glad that what I have written has given the opportunity to set the record straight.

My father? Well, he never was of any importance to the story and moreover what he ever knew of the whole thing was minimal. He was ignorant of virtually everything I have written down here; I didn't tell him, at the time, that I went to see Margaret Hooper; and, believe it or not, he never knew that I went on to look after the house! I did take him up to see the exhibition in London and, as far as it meant anything to him, it was that he'd done a clever thing putting me on to it. Not that the stuff was a patch on what he'd seen elsewhere.

And that just leaves me with me, quite literally. It's years that I've been thinking of doing this, believing it important, feeling I ought to. What a twist that I should end up, at one and the same time, seeing its insignificance, feeling the subject – and so much else – to be trivial to distress, and yet having clung to the writing the more this has become apparent. But now it is finished.

PART FOUR

XXII

And here I am. I had been told with professional calm and frankness, that my chances were not that great, and I seemed to accept this with mature resignation. After that, as we know, I had consciously sought to busy myself with a task become a futility – and the more appropriate for it. But that's hardly all of it, for a date with likely death in the operating theatre as, I imagine, a future time of execution, can have its own anaesthesia. An imminent danger of the sort would bring panic, the desire to go fighting and screaming, if only in the mind: with a set period of delay, shock becomes a normal state, a numb confusing opiate, bad things as good evade the grasp of thickened thoughts and, if anything, there is a desire for the resolution to be brought forward, to be over with.

My little tale did help, I suppose; I meandered but managed to pull myself along the main thread. There again, I seriously wonder whether the concentration on it – which wasn't easy – didn't stir up and draw with it all the incidental detail that encroached and which I was obliged to stem. Perhaps, ironically, if I had just let go, it might have been easier. But then, I don't know, I misgauged the ending by a mere fragment of a day and with writing the last line, with finishing in such a fine dogged way, I had only that time in which to wait for the hour.

But the worst – which I hadn't bargained for – was to come round, to find life still with me, and to realize that they were only *then* monitoring whether the operation was going to be a success or not. Perhaps they hadn't told me, perhaps it was meant to be obvious, perhaps it had eluded me (or I it), but I had naively thought I was either going to die on the operating table or, though less likely, I was going to awake, perhaps mending, but cured.

The situation I found myself in was the worst because I came to it *de nouveau*, unprepared, and because – even if I hadn't finished the story – I was in no state to successfully divert myself. No, I was in a wretched condition, groggy and nauseous to start with and then feeble, having to lie there, having to take whatever decided to enter my consciousness. The room I was in was a blank; I have no doubt it contained a known number of standard items, but it was all the more faceless for them. I was alone, not really even registering whether it was day or night. If there had been a clock then all I would have been aware of was its ticking. I didn't even have the energy to plug myself into the radio or ask for it to be done. The staff, of course, came and went but they were – and still are – ouside what I feel to be immediate. I don't know which is the worst, the well-meant familiarity put on with the uniform and activated at the door or the being seen to as something dehumanized, talked over, spoken about. There were no intellectual appeals at that stage – I wasn't up to it; some of what was said did get through to me, however, perhaps by a process akin to osmosis, and I was constantly aware of an ebb and flow of opinion the centre point of which was that it was 'touch and go'.

I would be lying if I said I could remember exactly what I thought of during those days – which I now know to have been two weeks. I know in general; it was all down to the story – the unimportant story – partly because it was no longer there to divert me but mostly because, as I have said, it had dragged up things which I thought I had left behind. All those 'incidentals' played out for me as though it was a rather bizarre show I was watching, and which I found compulsive.

Was I frightened of dying? Well, I was – not before the operation, for I had become attuned, but as I have implied, more strangely, after it when fettered with dreamlike inability I was in inescapable contact with it being 'touch and go'. But I have never been able to cope with the present, let alone the future, and the irony is that the extremity of the situation must have made some part of me attempt to escape into the coils of the past for respite. I was a step removed, watching in my mind's eye as muffled calls for my attention were made by my present plight, prospects and memories, all equally unwelcome.

This is just one interpretation, perhaps fanciful; well one doesn't know. More likely, more simply, it was that things that had been stirred up, which would have died with me, carried on in my consciousness when I survived. And I suppose another simple truth is that these things had drawn my attention as the story I was writing down seemed of less and less significance – the two were related. In the end, it was the incidental detail that I found of compelling interest, which I had to push back, and the tale which took persistence. It would also be true that I would seek refuge in the past as second nature but it must be said that the past (and truth) varies in the way one is at ease with it; it has layers, rather like an onion.

Even now I am playing the same game – and I know it. I am one, or more, layers down and I am certainly less at ease but it is like deliberately making oneself cry by the measured peeling of that onion. I succeeded in having too much on my mind even to contemplate whether there is a heart to the matter; it is easier to dig my fingernails into the palm of my hand. And, again, it means I avoid having to cope with the present and with the future. But there is something in me, some rebellious aggravating minor spirit or fragment of spirit, that is forcing me to say at this point – here, as I write – just where I am and what my situation is. I don't want to do it, but I'm going to; it is a perverse way of having some control over myself, like determinedly continuing that story to the end.

I am in hospital. I am in hospital in Ramsgate. And I'm dying. It was unexpected – well isn't it always? What I mean is that no matter how resigned I may be it still seems unjust; I'm not really that old – I'm only middle-aged, if that. My instinct is that there must be a mistake – but I know it isn't that sort of thing. We humans, in normality, feel that we control our lives and the world we live in, and it is a stark and essentially lonely experience to come against the unseen and unheeding greater and more elemental forces beyond the writ of our species. They are there and it is not at all uncommon for them to impinge – deaths, natural disasters, and the limitations imposed by reality are a part of everyday life but, collectively, we don't want to know. The music and babble may be momentarily dimmed but the party is soon resumed, few having noticed and with there being little trace of what happened; a tragedy, so keenly felt by those concerned, is a tiny, short-lived ripple in a limpid pool.

Death is the universal shocker at a personal level. One can try to ignore it, or inventively believe it to be a mere transition, but it always has been difficult to come to terms with simply as the end, the switching off. And there's no appeal. I mean, who can I complain to? And, whatever, what can be done? Nothing – it's a case of 'ready or not'. And, as I've always thought, death stands out as something there isn't any learning by. You can't watch someone else and say 'Ah' – or read a textbook. The sum total of deaths in history has not added a scruple beyond guesswork and contentious belief to understanding and knowledge. And it's not as though given second attempts an individual could do any better. I'm not being facile here for I've effectively died once – and I'm none the wiser for it. No, it's a great mystery and it doesn't help any that I feel it's as a black box which proves to have nothing inside. No, that doesn't help.

This scene must be played out endlessly – it is played out endlessly – but that doesn't help either. What does the faith of others do for me; or their lack of consciousness or sanity; or their being taken by surprise; or their beguiling the issue; or their being uncaring; or their being fearful? Where does it get me? Where did it get them?

I can half think of an analogy where there is no knowing whether the rules that are chosen are those that exist, where what the players do has no necessary effect on and connection with the outcome, and where the outcome – and all previous ones – remains forever unknown. But even half thinking of this is sufficient to expose how natural it is to build up a comforting complex structure from nothing, to assume there is something but that we don't know of it. It is all rather like hedgehogs weaving a rich mythology around the subject of getting run over.

I shouldn't laugh, it's not good for me. But then what is? And isn't that every reason for doing what the hell I like? But to be reduced to such a trivial and pointless compass of defiance and rebellion! My operation was a success – a complete success – and I got out of that room – even out of bed a bit – and I'm in the ward with others, a television, and a lot of clatter, goings on, routine, visitors, fruit, cards and flowers. Oh, but while the operation was such a 'success' it did nothing for the underlying heart disease. Well it wouldn't, would it? I had a rational and intellectual talk about this with the consultant and it was clear and obvious to both of us. I suppose it just made me more fit to die. I won't ever leave this place.

And I'm feeble, I'm so bloody feeble. When I talk about toying with the idea of whether to laugh or not it's in the context of now being able slowly to pad off by myself to the lavatory at the end of the room but of the floor upstairs being somewhere I couldn't contemplate going to alone. Nurses shave me, nurses bath me; I take medicines which I really 'have' to take. I live in pyjamas, dressing gown and slippers. I don't know where my clothes are, if I've still got any; I'll never need them.

At least I'm spared looking to friends and relations for help and understanding. It is so futile, so awfully futile really. I see it here at visiting time and – however played out – it is futile. They weep, they comfort, they are dully unaware, they are painfully bright and breezy, they bring bits and bobs, think of news, fidget – there is a whole catalogue of things that visitors do – and then they go. When you think about it there can be no possibility of any real help or any real understanding. I don't have friends and relations to come but even if I did I wouldn't want to tell them where I was. It's bad enough for me and it's bad enough on my own.

Oh, but let me be clear – it's different, of course, if you're going to get better. I'm sorry but that's simply a possibility that's not in my mind now. If you're not going to get better – as I am not or (I suspect) any in this ward with me – then you're effectively in a transit camp on the edge of the world of the living. Having awkward bits and pieces of that world blow in twice a day and blow back out again is rather like a seance in reverse.

No, I don't have any friends or relations – which the establishment is uneasy about. I'm used to it or, at least, I got used to it in fairly recent times. That is, not that I ever had a lot of friends or relations, but I let them slip when I moved back to Ramsgate. It seems funny to write it, but, that's it. They, the staff, keep trying to 'clarify my personal circumstances' in a gently intrusive way but we get to the end of the few questions they have on the form in their hand or mind's eye and I shake my head at the relevant times – quite truthfully, if in minimal response – and they are left with nothing, as I suppose, in that respect, I must be. No wife or girlfriend, no children, no living relative, no friends, no work, no one in social services (as they asked), and even what I'm holding back on them is pretty thin, consisting of a solicitor and a bank manager. There was a great moment – this going way back before my operation – when some bright young nurse produced a woman's earring that had been found in my jacket pocket. As I said, it had been dropped by a girl I once fortuitously shared a railway compartment with but who I hadn't known or spoken to and who I had never seen since. Nevertheless, that earring got pinned to a stand-up photo frame, its glass removed, and has subsequently followed me as of some intimate personal significance. It's on my locker now, and I like it.

That's something about this place – and I am telling you about this place – it has me in it but there's nothing of mine apart, perversely, from that earring. It's as though I've been stripped naked, divested of everything I've owned or been associated with and put in a totally sterile environment. I suppose that is exactly what's happened. The others do have one or two things – hairbrushes, their own night attire, slippers and dressing gown etc – but there isn't any more than will fill a carrier bag when I die, and there's a tendency for such things to be lifted up and cleaned under as though they are out of place. I've always been obsessed with possessions and so it's disturbing for me to be without them. I at least theoretically think what I refer to and am experiencing would be an interesting thing to do – an exercise, an experiment – but, really, not in the present circumstance.

And the same goes for the whole environment I now live in; it's all so very alien. The austere tidiness, the wipe-clean functional angularity, the materials, the smells, the pastel colours, the regime and the uniform. In many ways I might as well be on some giant docked space station; I certainly don't feel at home with my surroundings. I have tried sitting by the window and looking out, but the calculatedly winding asphalt paths over the carefully graded contours, the greenness checked on a shade chart, and the beds of transplanted vegetation put in growing medium for the duration of their desired usefulness – well, the least that can be said is that it is a suitable setting.

It is also very odd for me to be immersed in people – the other patients, their visitors, the staff. They don't say much in my direction but it is peculiar for me to have to be there in a captive sort of way, in a society which was hardly chosen – and where I am obliged to interact. As it happens, my neighbour is making all the characteristic signs of wanting to talk to me now. The tea trolley is coming and it's his opening. He talks endlessly of his life's experiences; frankly, he drives me scatty with boredom.

XXIII

It was rather fortuitous how the completely unexpectable request to caretake the old house coincided with the final demise of my life in Cambridge. Perhaps I have conveyed much by having said so little on the subject.

My 'job', in fact dependant on joining up a continuous series of small jobs, disappeared when the economic climate caused the flow of funding to falter. This happened before – and during – the last visits to Ramsgate that I mentioned. It wasn't that I was sacked or that I suddenly left for good so much as I ceased to have a reason to go in and it, unexpectedly, stayed that way for what might be called the relevant period – and I never went back.

The situation inevitably brought with it feelings of uncertainty and loss of self-esteem and being squeezed, worthless, out of what I did added that bit to – or was added to by – a growing disenchantment with archaeology as a profession. Mind you, it is difficult to continue to believe in an occupation as a profession when you find your grasp and incorporation to have been so slender and fanciful. I think I actually would have rallied – you know how one picks oneself up and rationalizes – had it not been for the 'tomb', which had brought back the long dulled zest of early acquaintance to me, the buzz that had first captured. And then – probably more importantly – there was the house; a magnificent let-out and an enticement in its own right – and so terribly opportune.

I'd always thought of what I 'did' to be what I wanted to do – and to have been a fought for achievement. But I took no convincing, the opportunity set before me, that it had to be easier to fulfil oneself without frustration and without being confined to a narrow hacked-out route.

There was freedom on offer and nowhere was this more apparent than with my then marriage – which is a subject that even now, or particularly now, I really don't like to dwell on. It had not worked out, to say the least; any affection had proved superficial, there was a complete lack of sympathy – or do I mean empathy – and it had got terribly twisted, and bitter, and sniping, and enmeshing, and nightmarish, and – most of all – a waste of life. Losing my work didn't help, one way or another. Oh, I relive the release that that house represented as I write this. And it gave it that little twist that it must have been her (my wife) that let on to my father what I'd been up to with the house, over the phone, in one of those behind my back calls. This made sense of my father suddenly having come up with the subject, though I never asked either of them if it was the case.

So I decided to move to Ramsgate, and I left Cambridge behind with a glad heart and with relish for what I was going to. Of course, as the matter of the imagined telephone call alone demonstrated, the two places were connected – by my own connections – and it would have been fain to have disappeared in one and broadcast my presence in the other. Not, as it happens, that I had any desire to live an open and outward life in Ramsgate. Quite the reverse, for I wanted to use the opportunity to retreat – in the philosophical sense – to put myself out of the way of old ties, commitments and constraints, to reflect, rest, and find my own direction. The curatorship of the house itself also had implications in harmony with my desire but which were, in any case, unavoidable.

All in all I was headed, knowingly and willingly, towards seclusion and isolation. And it was this set of circumstances – plainly and obviously – that meant that I dropped former contacts and relationships, and which is why I am now so starkly without them. There is, however, a perhaps strange aspect of that . . . this . . . the situation which I think bears some drawing out. You see, it is rather odd to leave one's place of birth, where one grew up, a place with which there has been a continuing if degraded association, and then to return in the persona of someone with no connection there, or presumed different connections.

Analogies and metaphors fail me but it has been an experience akin to finding myself in a coexisting dimension, looking in as an outsider, while being able to make a fresh start in a familiar land but independent of my former self there. While, as I have said, my father never knew about my looking after or living in the house (or my having moved to Ramsgate), I continued to see him from time to time and he was thus a blemish or fault between two planes of my spatial existence. James was also a potential problem in this respect but I feel that I would be jumping ahead of the flow of what I want to relate if I more than merely mentioned either of them here. The point I wish to convey is that I became a stranger in my own country – and that that country became a very strange one in turn.

I took a lot of things with me, in a small removal van, which I drove myself; it's amazing what you can hire on an ordinary driving licence. Makes me wonder what else I could have hired in my time. But, anyway, unlike with other such removals, I didn't bring the contents of a household, lock, stock and barrel: I had no need, desire or right. What I brought – ruffling as few feathers as possible, but being more firm than I perhaps ever had been – were objects with associations that were personal to me. There were some bits and pieces of furniture; there were books – a lot of books; and an unexpectedly large number of odds and ends – objects and papers – detritus and knickknacks with memories. It was all an odd assortment, reminding one not so much of what might have been selected in a house clearance as of what might have been left over. I also brought the more mundane things – clothes, bedding, food – practical things one would need in the circumstances. I think I even made a list, like going camping. What I didn't bring was anything to do with work – it may all be there yet – or any of the accumulation of the years that was not a part of me. What I didn't leave was anything of myself.

I'd burnt my bridges and I must confess to having had, not qualms, but a feeling of panic on getting to Ramsgate. I wasn't going to drive right up to the nursing home, it seemed inappropriate, and, besides, I wanted to change the momentum and not burst in still travelling. So I parked outside the house, because I was tired of the journey as far as the van went, and it was also the right distance to give me a walk. There was then one of those defined moments in the flow of time when contact with reality is much more immediate than normal, as though an undetectable screen has been removed. There I was, me and my capsule of possessions, alongside the kerb, in the public road; and there was the house I had thrown up everything to come to, on the other side of the hedge, and doubtless heavily secured by the forces of law and order. I had no title whatsoever. Right, Mrs Hooper had said and, true, it had sounded as though it would work, and, yes, I was going to see her just now – and was expected. But her letter confirming the appointment made no mention of what it was about (and nor had mine to her); what was proposed might be legally laughable and impossible, and there was certainly nothing at all on paper. Though it seemed otherwise, she may not have been of her right mind, or she may have changed her mind, or she may have offered something not in her power – or she may have died or become comatose. I had been precipitant and a hot and cold flush went over me – but I need not have worried.

There she was, perhaps imperceptibly more faded than when I last saw her, and with that kind of frail vitality that was characteristic. On having asked, I had been shown into a small sitting-room and I was aware of preparedness and, if you like, of being 'received'. Visitors were quite a subject at the Dunbarry Nursing Home – in a different way from my present situation – and not only, one felt, was Margaret Hooper having me, but – as noteworthy – it warranted the use of that room. It was like getting the best china out and, indeed, the best china was out, on a trolley, with an electric kettle by it. The chintz-covered suite was homely but had high firm seats, there were a few unpossessed ornaments and pictures but no personal clutter, and a vase of flowers had been put in and the room aired. It reminded me of the removal van I had just left; Margaret Hooper had effectively hired a sitting-room.

'When did you travel down?' she asked, smiling, and adding, 'Do sit down.'

I was amused by the question on the lips of one of the older generation; it bespoke more leisured times, though part of my amusement was in my anticipation of being able, personally, to take things more at my own pace.

'Oh, I got here with a good half hour to spare,' I answered. 'I drove all my things down in a van and parked it outside the house and walked round.'

'Well I had wondered whether you would change your mind,' she said. 'But I hoped not – and I felt you wouldn't – and I am glad you are here. As you've brought everything with you in a van there hardly seems any point in asking whether you are sure of what you're doing.'

'I'm certain,' I responded. I didn't mention any worries I'd had on her account but I did say, 'I'd be in more than a bit of a pickle if it all didn't happen now. I've just taken it as a certainty since we first agreed.'

'Quite!' Margaret was emphatic. 'And everything is in order. I've been hard at work,' she gave me a smile and chuckle, 'and my solicitor – our solicitor – will be here in half an hour. I arranged it that way, and well, I dare say you could do with a cup of tea just now . . .'

I demurred; the tray was set for three.

'I arranged it this way,' she continued, 'because I wanted to give you some of the private background to the situation. The more I've thought about it the more I've come to the conclusion that it's only fair and that it will make the whole thing more readily understandable. The solicitor knows little,' she looked at me, 'his father who originally handled it all died a while back anyway – and the young one's uninquisitiveness is, I feel, based less on inherited discretion than ignorance and, well, not being the same man. It's best if we leave it that way with him but I've thought through what I want to tell you.' Saying this, she put on a pair of reading glasses and unfolded a sheet of writing paper that had been under their case. It had a few notes scribbled on it.

'I ran off from home when I was twenty-one to marry an Irishman. I'd met him at a dance and he wasn't considered at all suitable – oh dear me no. He was of the wrong religion, the wrong class, he had no connections or money and, of course, my father had been in the military and the Free State was, in any case, a bad subject in the run up to the war. They wouldn't have him at the house and scolded me terribly when they knew he'd been seeing me for months; plans to send me abroad were put into immediate action! But I loved my Niall, he was so handsome and so clever and considerate. Oh . . .' Margaret paused in thought. 'So I went off on their blooming old trip, got out at London with all my baggage and wrote a note home. There must have been a terrible furore – things are quite different these days – but I never knew because I never went back to see. That was out of the question – as we always joked, I'd certainly put myself beyond the pale!'

The joke fell flat on me, but she went on.

'I had travelling money and I also had money to purchase clothes from the Army and Navy – which I didn't buy. This gave us a start and we rented a flat, Niall got a job, and we were married. Start, flat, job and wedding would all have shocked my parents horribly but that was part of the charm of it; it wasn't at all what I was used to – the delicious, fresh, simple pleasures of roughing it! But those were wonderful days, wonderful, I could go on for ever and we have very little time.'

I said I'd be back and that she could tell me at greater length. I'd be very interested. I was interested too, and I might have wondered why.

'I haven't been able to tell anyone, you know,' she said sadly. 'To go on, it was a bubble of pleasure that was soon burst. Things came to a head with the "phoney war"; we'd managed not to notice until then but it wasn't easy being Irish in London at that time. Niall – bless him – he wasn't at all militaristic and his own government was keeping out, but there were pressures and it wasn't as though he could get in a reserved occupation, his ability to keep in any employment was on the line. All this got to him dreadfully and it became muddled up with the hard times that were beginning to hit us and, in some perverse way, with his doing what he imagined my parents would have wanted. Anyway, he joined up – Royal Irish Volunteers – and it was a terrible, awful mistake. I could tell from between the lines of his letters how desperately unhappy and almost mentally deranged he was. I didn't push him into joining – I didn't want him to go – but I should have spoken out more; it wasn't him and I still blame myself. Still, to this day. Well the letter came, not the killed one, not the recorded as having been taken prisoner, but the missing in action. And I stayed in limbo for he never was confirmed as having been killed or as having been captured.'

She was getting tearful. I didn't know what to do. I would have known later on in our relationship. But there was a knock on the door, and I was glad of it.

XXIV

It was the solicitor. Balding, bespectacled, with a suit and briefcase, making an entrance.

'Ah, Mrs Hooper, I came a few minutes early in case you wished to speak to me, but I see Mr Riley is here; well and good.'

He shook hands with me while adjusting his glasses.

'We can get off to a start then. Yes, Mr Riley, Mrs Hooper and I have had a long discussion about what might be termed the personal circumstances of this matter. My firm has drawn up the papers, so it's merely a matter of a few signatures in the right place now.' He laughed; he was nervous, jerky, inadequate.

I made the tea and signed where I was told to. Staff came in and witnessed, or at least they too signed as instructed. It was all genteel and proper, though with an air of complexity made simple; there were a number of forms and signatures, with pages being turned over, crosses put here and there, the attention of different people being called, papers being put away and with the solicitor saying as he thought appropriate that 'it is just the fact that these people have signed that you are being asked to witness'.

I noticed that the staff tended to smile at me in a kindly way when their eye caught mine or vice versa. I also noticed – though the solicitor was definitely trying to keep it from view – that the papers were not in the name of Margaret Hooper but of Margaret Elspeth Creswell, and her husband Edmund Albert Cresswell. Then there was the content of what was being signed for – which I caught the spirit of, and which truly astonished me – not that I could say anything. I had expected some control over the house but what I was getting – for what it was worth – was power of attorney over all and sundry in the old woman's lifetime and – it appeared – her estate on her death.

At the time, and given the circumstances, it seemed natural to me that I knew less than I might have. And, in point of fact, as soon as the solicitor had ushered the witnesses out, he apologized for the haste saying we 'wouldn't want everyone knowing our business', and then he summarized the whole scheme of things in as clear a manner as he was capable of. But, again, I could say nothing since it was apparent that he thought I'd known all; what he was doing was reiterating in order to lay out how he had discharged what had been required of him. And it helped him effect his exit smiling and, I felt, being somewhat familiar with me. Mind you, it was catching, for I thanked him as though I had had a part in his instruction.

Margaret and I were left rather like a blushing couple. 'Let me finish,' she said, 'or I'll lose the thread of my story.'

'I was getting tearful, wasn't I? Well, I still do when I think back on Niall going missing.' Oddly, she then smiled in a happy way. 'It was terrible, the little world I'd got into was built around him, and it was a solace that turned painful to keep things as they were over months of declining hope and never hearing. I could work and did work – under my maiden name as a clerical assistant in a hospital – but I was going downhill and in the end I took the chance of being transferred here to Ramsgate. It wasn't the Dunkirk business – well after; people never understand, but it turned out to be part of the back-up for the Normandy Invasion. It was a bit of sea air and a change for me, it did me good and I stayed on till after the war ended, long enough to be sure that Niall was never coming back.

'And I met a man, as one does, at a "social" – a dance – and I ended up being asked, with the crowd I was on the fringes of, to a party at his house. That was Eddy Creswell. No one knew him, he'd just arrived in Ramsgate but there were a lot of people "passing through", particularly in our business, and friendships were easily struck up and they as easily left no trace. Let me see, how can I describe Eddy when I first met him? He was gay – oh dear, yes, that meant, then, that he was cheerful and lively; he was flush – and free with his money; and he was dapper – well turned out, well-dressed, smart clothes and all that. It was a tonic in post-war Britain, I can tell you, land of the free, land of rationing and promises! He was a charmer too, a bit of a ladies' man, but not over the top, and he was also a man's man in a superior sort of way, keeping what he'd been up to close to his chest. He was a strange mixture of someone who had to be "in" while at the same time being aloof and separate. I don't think anyone "knew" him; I never did.' She stopped. 'Not boring you am I?'

I smiled, 'Not a bit.' I was, I must say, thinking at the back of my mind about moving in, and getting the van back.

'Well, his house, as you've no doubt guessed, is the one you'll be moving into when I let you get away. It had been called Manorhouse before it was India House. It's a piece of the past now, isn't it, but it was even then, so colonial, so full of all those wonderful things everywhere. Oh! I love that house, you know,' she said. 'We were the younger generation and while we weren't beatniks there was a feeling of being let loose in someone's grandparents' house. Eddy had inherited it as it stood, and had moved from abroad to take it up – and he felt the same way. It had belonged to an uncle he didn't know who'd retired there from a post with the Colonial Service; it was a matter of the other branches of the family tree having been lopped off that it came to Eddy. He didn't have any relatives that he knew of. Anyway, was that house lively among the cobwebs! It wasn't quite as bad as a château occupied by troops but, certainly after the first excitement, I began to feel that way. Mind, some of the glass-rings and cigarette burns are still there and I actually got to like them. And then there's the piano; we never knew how it got upstairs, and we never understood why it didn't end up on the floor below!

'I don't remember Eddy that clearly now, I suppose the bit of his character that counted was his liveliness. I suppose the time I'm talking about also wasn't that long, and it's a long time ago, and it all became rather eclipsed and suppressed. I'm sorry, I am. I'm sure I must have loved Eddy at the time and he certainly seemed to be totally taken up with me. He asked me to marry him just when I found I'd fallen pregnant – how's that for timing? Niall was gone, I was only known under my maiden name, it was a crime but . . . that was the situation. We were married in the registry office and none of my family knew – I had no contact with them – and we didn't know any of his family. As far as I could see there was no harm.'

She looked at me directly, turned her head to the window, and went on. 'It was early in my second marriage – when I met Niall, the husband who I had presumed dead. It was very sudden, we virtually walked into each other in the town – and I collapsed with the shock. It turned out that the army – or the war – had proved too much for Niall. Things had been so-so until he was involved in something unspeakably nasty, poor man. His unit had overrun a fuel depot which proved to be booby-trapped, and which was then retaken. I couldn't come near to understanding how dreadful the experience had been –

the horror of it was always there for him – and its immediate effect was to make him run off, crazed. No one knew he'd deserted – he was missing in action, presumed a prisoner or an unidentifiable corpse – but he didn't know that. To Niall, he was on the run and after he'd made it back to Ireland he kept very low. He didn't think I'd want to know him and, besides that, he thought they'd be waiting for him. He was crazy anyway, and I wasn't with him. He missed me. He apparently did end up writing to me in London but by then I'd gone, and the flat had been bombed. As soon as the war ended he, circumspectly, came looking for me – it's only from him I know that the flat was bombed – and we put two and two together regarding the letters. He found out I'd "gone down to Ramsgate" through the casual half-truthful enquiries he felt he was able to make and then he'd simply come down here and hung around on the chance of seeing me, not knowing whether I'd moved on. And then, bang, I fainted at the sight of him.

'But when I came to, I knew who I loved. There was me, remarried to another man, pregnant by another man, but I knew who I loved and I couldn't keep it back. At the same time, coming back to consciousness, I knew that I had to tell Niall what the situation was as soon as possible. I got up, thanking strangers, and bade Niall follow me with my eyes; he then supported me in a bittersweet walk, a few hundred yards that took forever and seemed so fleeting. He blamed himself, it was all he deserved; I told him it wasn't his fault, that I cared for him, but that I didn't know what to do with the conflicting loyalties I had; we agreed to meet.

'We actually met every week after real or invented ante-natal appointments; the days between were dead, the day itself over-brimming with insufferable emotion. And I was growing, week by week, like some sort of bomb that would explode. We were spotted by the doctor and by two of the other mothers: they said they had seen me with Mr Creswell! That time, those hours, the whole situation was both wonderful and wretched and it can't have helped with what happened with the real Mr Creswell. That's an understatement, oh dear, I still feel guilty, I really do. Eddy was going to pieces. There was a man who thrived on excitement and activity and he increasingly felt imprisoned – he had the house, but not the sort of money he needed, and he felt he was trapped in a backwater, got more and more morose, and drank in bouts. I was part of the problem and he would certainly binge when he couldn't cope with a wife who was racked by emotion and who was unreachable and inattentive: marriage, family life, and commitments became spectres to him. When he was in the grips of such drunken mood swings he would talk of "selling up to release capital", of "going back to Africa, with or without you" and the like. Whatever the rights and wrongs, I found this very threatening and when he offered me security in his alternate moods of (equally drunken) affection and remorse I didn't say no. This was how the house, the investments, and the bank account got to be in joint names; it wasn't usual in those days.

'And then, to cut a long story short, I came back from one of my meetings with Niall – I was eight months' pregnant – and there was no Eddy. I called for him and, after a while, I looked over the house; I assumed he'd gone out – though that was something he very rarely did. But he didn't come back so I naturally began to wonder whether he'd cleared off. I was still alone when it came time to go to bed, and he didn't come the next day, or the day after. I was sorry, I really was, because I did care for him and I would have made enquiries except that I felt in a very difficult position, though I did go through the local newspaper. In any case, he had talked of going, and I couldn't help working through how I would manage – checking that all the financial papers were where they should be, though also finding his possessions untouched. That third evening I thought of the cellar and there he was, at the bottom of the steps that used to lead to it, stone dead. He'd often gone down there – I dare say he had a bottle or two hidden – I don't know why I didn't think of it before.

'I suppose if I had found him straight off I would have gone to the police. As it was I'd had time to think and I was, besides, seriously rattled. I wasn't legally married to Eddy, I'd committed a crime, Niall was alive, I was in danger of not having a roof over my head and I was about to give birth to a child who would be illegitimate. And then there was the situation with Niall, who was very much alive and had been seen and thought to be Eddy by the doctor. He would be discovered, that would itself be threatening and, in my blackest thoughts, I wondered what might be made of me not finding the body and of it looking as much, as they say, as if Eddy might have been pushed as he'd fallen.

'The body itself didn't worry me, once I knew that was where he was and how he was. I have to say that in a way it was a relief, not that I would have wished it, but that it resolved the irresolvable, like cutting the Gordian knot. And as the consequences were more what I was worried about I closed the cellar door, didn't panic, thought long and hard and, the week up, met Niall after my next supposed ante-natal clinic. Again, to cut a long story short, he too saw providence and fate hand in hand, fell in with what I had thought out, and came to occupy India House with me as Edmund Creswell. He was even, in the end, buried as Edmund Creswell, or his ashes were.'

'And the skeleton in the tomb,' I volunteered, 'is the real Edmund Creswell.'

'Just so,' she said, 'but there was no disrespect, I can assure you. It was a very fine mausoleum I understand and, as the second Eddy said, it was fitted up as for a king. He cleaned it and swept it with the greatest care – took all the junk out, he put those objects you're so interested in down there and removed anything that might indicate the body didn't belong with them. Then Eddy-Niall sealed it up, continuing the floor over the stair and that, we supposed, was that. We didn't know anything about this passage from the sea you went up.'

'Strictly speaking,' I ventured, 'the house and everything else you've given me power of attorney over – it doesn't belong to you, does it?'

'Strictly speaking,' she said, 'but no one knows that and no one ever will know it. Not now. After the first Eddy died I did all the signing and when the second Eddy went I was, of course, his widow and all the joint property went to me automatically. So that was that for all anyone knows. And it was all perfectly fine except the money side of things got tighter and tighter and when I wasn't able to look after myself any more I had to come here and I had a real problem. I couldn't sell the house – I didn't want to – because of the first Eddy being there but I couldn't afford all the costs involved in keeping it up. I've been able to less and less. So I shut the house up and I agreed with the doctor to move in here on the understanding that I did so in my maiden name and quite anonymously. I didn't expect to live this long and the worry of the house has got to be such a burden. You see how you can help but the reason I only mentioned the house to you is that the rest amounts to very little, scarcely more I understand than will keep me, though that will come to you. I hope I should have told you what I have, there was actually no need for you to know, but it seemed right. Well?'

'It's a lot for me to take in,' I answered truthfully, 'but it will be OK.' I felt it had to be made OK. 'But what about your child?' I asked.

At this the tears welled in her eyes again. 'That wasn't to be; it was probably as well. What about Eddy's bones? Do what you like with the things but I would like the bones to go back, if you're there to look after it all.'

I nodded and she looked content. The meeting had evidently been a drain on both of us but I think we came out of it feeling we were on the same side.

XXV

Still here. I could say a little bit older, but that doesn't seem right, for the time now doesn't go past in hours for me, so much as in large segments of the unknown remainder of my days. Do I as a person get less, I wonder? Margaret did, as she became more and more at one with her memories and with her life as a whole but she, unlike me, was old. James was cut down, fully alive one minute and dead the next, but apart from the fact that his death was sudden – unanticipated by him or anyone else – he had hardly reached the stage of looking forward, let alone that of looking back. Oh yes, and I have been put on some different medication: I suppose that passes for news.

James' death happened early on; I found out about it the first time I went to my father's. That visit bristled with difficulties, even more than before; frankly, to the point of impossibility. I don't regret for a moment never letting him know I'd moved back to Ramsgate; it was wise, very wise. I don't know why I went there but – from a theoretical point of view – he was my father and we had ourselves as we were and our relationship going back into the past. It's sad as I write it, partly because of the reality of it, but also because I had spent so long – and so much anguish – in not recognizing or coming to terms with that reality.

I remember that first occasion I went there 'from London'. He'd been unwelcoming, unenthusiastic, unenquiring, he'd touched upon as many points of aggravation as could be reasonably expected; and he'd obliquely made sure that a number of my perceived inadequacies were still where he'd left them. And then he said about 'that boy you started to knock around with, James'. He'd been found at the bottom of the cliff. 'I'll bet his parents won't want to see you!'

I'd been going to go up there too. I'm talking here about very shortly after I'd moved back to Ramsgate and, having considered the matter, I decided to let James in on the whole thing, but to play it by ear a bit and first make contact again when I was 'down from London'.

Dead! – it mentally winded me; I don't even remember anything between hearing this and arriving at James' parents' house.

Well, James had been buried. 'Just a small family affair like' but this was said to indicate the eschewed possibility of something grander and not out of any animosity. The impression given was that I was one among a series of anticipated callers who, like me, would be treated with the front room courtesy and propriety which was felt appropriate. Raw uncontrolled grief – or anything like it – if it had been, had been replaced by a dignified acceptance which was worn well.

'You know, Jonathan,' Ted said, when I had been arranged, 'Cath and I are glad now that James spent the time he did helping you in Cambridge.'

'Of course, it meant we were without him for that bit,' said Cathy.

'But we're agreed that he did something useful and – I make no pretence – I wasn't sure at the time he wouldn't have been better doing something else, but now it's good that he did a little of what he fancied. Isn't it Cath?'

Cathy, looking tearful but cheerful, agreed. 'Yes, that's what Ted and I think. Though his interests went back a long way' (... i.e. long before me ...) 'to when he was much smaller.'

James' mother was actually crying, his father's ready hand upon her shoulder, as – following her direction – I got up to look in a cabinet.

'We couldn't keep everything,' she said.

'No, no, wouldn't be healthy,' Ted explained.

'But we went through what he'd collected for a few momentos,' she continued.

Strange little collection of the more perfect and decorative. And, more to the point, an odd association as they'd been scarcely aware of the objects during their son's life, had an obvious antipathy towards that sort of thing themselves, didn't know what they were, and wouldn't know where they came from. But I recognized that what was in there had been made safe, handleable, OK, suitable, by encapsulation in (from my viewpoint) a mediocre, modern, veneer, banged together – though not inexpensive – cabinet, doubtless bought for the purpose. The metalwork and coins must have been polished with a metal drill attachment, the pottery was squeaky clean (and probably bleached), there was nothing at all dirty. What about things that were too small or too large, or were broken, or didn't suit the arrangement? What indeed about everything else? I didn't ask. Good job James never took anything from the tomb that way.

'That really is quite charming,' I said. They smiled back, gratified, glancing at each other, pressing each other's hand.

'It will help,' Ted said. 'Of course, James has gone now but it's Cathy and I that have to live on. I've always said that, haven't I Cath? I've always said that it's them that survives that has it worst. It's not obvious that though, is it?'

I agreed that what he was saying wasn't obvious but I felt that a photo of the two of them – in the role that had come to them – with the small cabinet-shrine in the background would – if I'd taken it that instant – have said it all. They looked like a pair of minor deities or saints portrayed with their emblems. Being parents hadn't fitted but bereavement gave an easeful importance.

The occasion wasn't for me, I couldn't get anything out of it; I had been looking for something, but I left feeling hollow and empty. There was the relationship between James and his parents – not that that mattered a tinker's to me; and there was the relationship between me and James – not that that was actually very important either. But what I felt, in both respects, was the dreadful suddenness. I could say it was an issue of things unsaid, though it was not – for in neither case, I imagine, was there anything much to say. But, again, it was the suddenness, the fact that settling matters, however – and even if unnecessary or undesired – was denied.

I made a good exit from the Stones' and had no doubt that, to them, my visit was – well – as it should have been. I could imagine the bland, clichéd, but safely favourable comments as the china was washed, dried, and put away. 'Nice', 'nice', 'nice'. Although I'd told my own father I had to go straight to London (not even via James') I went back to his house. James' death – and the visit to his parents – had rattled me and, somehow, I wanted to talk, to talk as a son with his father.

Looking back, I suppose I'd always avoided the issue and I think that, even in attempting not to do it, I have – in writing – introduced a greater perception in this regard than existed. That evening was a turning point, or a point of no return. I didn't hide, I didn't pretend, I didn't delude myself; I tried, persistently, to talk to my father. I tried, and I tried, and I tried. And I got absolutely nowhere. It was only then that I realized – and it's hard for me to credit this too – that it was only then that I realized that there was no point of contact, no avenue of real communication, no genuine interest. There was this thing in a chair, its apparent form revealed in a science-fiction way to be nothing but a negative field which had effectively deterred examination. I left, and was left with, an infinitely greater feeling of emptiness than when I had been at James'; it went to the root of my being.

I did go back to see my father, in fact I went back many times or, at least, I went as often as I ever had from Cambridge, about once a month, though not staying the night. But it could never be the same; I suppose that's obvious and I am not saying it out of any regret – dear me, no – only to make the point. Whether it was better or worse is debatable, but it was certainly different. I would go along there, actually starting amused by really having walked along the road, and all that had previously stung and hurt and had its grip came over as comic, irrelevant, sad or – at most – contemptible. I didn't bother to answer back, or explain, or solicit interest, but stuck to smiling platitudes and superficial everyday concerns, even making a game of it and simply edging off at the slightest sign of real contact of any sort.

What did my father make of the change? Well, I have to say that in a way he didn't notice – that is that my fundamentally changed attitude to him, the fact that I had seen through it all, none of this registered at all. But I am being pedantic here, or humorous, or something, for he certainly saw the change – albeit gradually – from his own standpoint. He didn't say anything – that would have been too generous – but he saw me 'growing up at last', 'settling down a bit', 'not being difficult', 'having a respect for his age', and so on. But the main benefit for him was that it was easy, with no demands of the sort that bewildered him or left him unresponsive. It was a bit of company, perhaps on a level with a 'do-gooder' coming round but more acceptable than that, and a debt repaid (to him); even if I did have to listen to his complaints about how families weren't what they used to be!

But what was in it for me? Superficially a distressing problem relationship had been resolved – hooray – but once I'd tumbled, I was the last person to see things this way – 'Ooh, they do get on well now' – and I have difficulty even writing the proposition down. What I ended up with was a fairly lobotomised, shallow, unrewarding relationship with an old man who was my father in a way that didn't mean very much – I don't know, like someone might be a second cousin twice removed (who wasn't my type). There was no difficulty to it, but there was no spark or point any more either. And I suppose the meaninglessness of it all not only bored me – I'm a person who thrives on stimulus – but visit by visit, and between visits, it brought to my attention not only what I didn't have, but what I had never had (and never would).

I was on my own and taking away this sham relationship – and I include both my parents here – I, rather frighteningly, always had been. Even when I was very small, and in all those years of growing. I may have neutralized something, got rid of it, but in so doing was left with myself, past and present. No wonder I went off down the trails I did between then and now, no wonder, but I will come to that. It is relevant to say that other things were going on in my life and through my brain from the time I moved to Ramsgate to my father's death and that these both fed off and fuelled the irreversible wasting to nothingness of that relationship.

As I'm sitting here awaiting death in such an organized setting, propped comfortably on pillows (writing pad on my knees, glasses on nose) and regularly serviced and monitored – and particularly as I have spoken about James going, as it were, without proper notice – I suppose I should say something about my father in this respect. I know I don't have to but do I want to?; can I?; is there anything much to relate? He didn't die of anything in particular, it was 'cardiac failure' on the certificate – I see my own death certificate there – but in his case it was old age really; if it hadn't been one thing it would have been another. I noticed him going downhill over time but I didn't say anything: if he knew – at any stage – he wouldn't have said anything to me. There were no solaces, meaningful conversations, or sortings out or partings. Even nearing the last . . . He had to go into a hospital – actually another part of this hospital – because I was his only relative and I lived in London and could only come down occasionally. Even then we chose to ignore the issue as people affect 'not to know' a person, often finding themselves convincing.

I have no reason for not being honest and can say that visiting my father became increasingly tedious and pointless. That's from my point of view and I must say that the whole episode did nothing to provoke or promote thought in me. For him it was always as though someone from meals-on-wheels (but who he could square up to) had arrived; and as for thinking, well, in the sense I mean, he didn't. One day I went there – or, rather, here – and there was an empty bed. He'd only recently died. They'd tried to get hold of me on the London number I'd given. 'Would I like to see him?' 'No,' I said, 'I wouldn't.' Looking at the empty bed – already changed and pristine – for the few minutes I was there was enough and sufficient for me.

I'd taken in a few of those things that people never want or need – and my father never wanted or needed anything I could give him – and I hung around for his possessions. But I only did this because I felt I should. I put the lot in a bin at the first opportunity I could do so unobserved. And – on a larger scale – I did much the same with my father's house and its contents. There was nothing of me there and I made nothing of what there was, not even keeping a photograph. I don't want to convey any hurt or upset, there may have been some vestige but what there was most of was nothing.

XXVI

Damnation, I've caught some sort of cold – and colds, however minor, always go to my chest so. Still, I'm in the right place! But I hate that unstayable feeling that leads on to coughing up all sorts of odious matter. It's just a cold, I know, but they always made me feel worse than they warrant. I suppose it's because I was such a weakly child spending endless and nightmarish periods in bed. Brings back memories of being on my own, feeling ill, fearful, lonely, I've always put my subsequent making much of colds down to this; it's the reliving of a child's emotions of terror, panic and desertion. And I do feel decidedly chesty in a horrible wet and wheezy way with this cold, it's awful. It's awful, I can't describe it. Come to that, I can't describe much, I'm finding writing really difficult, but I'll go back and correct this later.

I must press on, I must. I don't like being in this place, it makes me feel exposed – that is, that I don't have any context, like some animal that's been taken out of its rich little environment and put in a naked concrete yard. Writing helps me cocoon myself. And I don't like being ill, I never did, and while always seemingly making much of it, I was always inwardly hiding, closing my eyes, pretending it wasn't there. And as for knowing that I'm dying, well, I'm not pretending there but I'm not doing anything else either. I mean, what can you do? I am writing and that is a diversion. I did start out writing to communicate, to leave something, to inform, to explain. But I am not now. That most important of archaeological finds (it's almost as though I'm copying out these words without feeling or understanding) seems so entirely unimportant. And what is important is something that I can't grasp. But even if I could I'm not sure I'd want to tell anyone. No, if I'm trying to communicate, then I'm trying to communicate with myself; I'm turning things over to inform and explain, but only for me. Largely just turning things over, or casting my net in the hope of catching something. But why write things down for myself? I don't know. Maybe to make me think in a measured and structured way.

There's so much that I don't know but one thing I am as sure of as not liking it here is that I liked the house. Liking is a weak word, strangely – or perhaps not so strangely – I found myself there, as in my inner self. You see – or, rather, I see – that I am using the past tense. That reminds me of Margaret; she knew she was never going there again. Margaret, the house, which shall I start with? The house.

I don't know quite where I got to writing down what the formalities of it were, and I can't be bothered to look. In fact, I've never looked back over any of what I have written and, just now, I don't think I could get it out of the locker. But Margaret never had any legitimate right to the house. It was the fruits of a bigamous marriage, a marriage which she perpetuated by substituting her first husband for her second when the latter died. Part of where I came in was to keep that secret for her time, the fear of it coming out otherwise haunting her as she took unavoidable refuge within the nursing home, the house so vulnerable and beyond her protection. Also, of course, the house meant a good deal to her and I set her mind at rest about it being simply vandalized – an appropriate word – the time before my moving in being largely dealt with by white lies on my part and a suspension of disbelief on hers. But apart from keeping secrets and preventing destruction, I always felt there was another reason why I was there. There had to be another reason. However, that aside, as I lie here I am stuck in a similar position to the one she was in.

I say similar, and I suppose superficially it is. But I'm not in perpetual fear of having awkward questions asked – and accusations made – about a dead body. Though I do wonder what I'll say if it comes to it. Between me and this page, I was never entirely sure about the death of Margaret's second husband – whether he really fell, or whether he was indeed pushed. I was never sure and in a way it didn't matter, but in another the death, either way, and the so visible body, gave me a strange feeling.

When I moved into the house I immediately started to put things to rights and I did this with an instinctive enthusiasm which didn't abate. I'm sure it's a job that could never be finished, though I got sufficiently far to feel satisfied rather than disappointed now on that account.

Having said that I 'put things to rights' it occurs to me that most people would take this as something quite different, that it would not be interpreted as I mean. No, I didn't hire anyone to 'clear out' the house – nor did I do it myself – packing all the poor broken contents into skips at the door, emptying, getting rid of the rubbish, clearing the decks. No, I didn't do that and I didn't get 'back to basics' by throwing out carpets and stripping wallpaper and paint; I didn't do this either. Nor did I have the house 'looked at' from the point of view of structural work that needed doing – nor, come to that, did I bother myself with the likes of rewiring, damp-proofing, or central heating. Had I taken this route then the house as a structure would have been made as near new as possible, I would have decorated to my taste, and I would have furnished it similarly.

I mention this not merely to clear up a misunderstanding – to point out the difference between my understanding and the generality – but also to outline what would have happened normally – horror of horrors – and, indeed, what will happen when I go. Now, that has made me upset: I'll put it to the back of my mind and think about it later. The point now is if the above isn't what I meant then what did I do? What I did – or what I attempted to do – was to put the house back as it had been when it was first left. (And at that time, it must be appreciated, it had been kept much as it always had been.)

So what I did initially with the debris in each room was not to throw it out but to pore over it and sort it out. I tried, gradually, to put everything back in place – as one might, for example, after a burglary. There was, naturally, much that was broken or ruined, of which I made a mental note, and then, of course, there were intrusive objects – which I got rid of sharply – and there was what was missing. The whole problem of decoration, etc I approached just as though I was spring-cleaning. I shampooed carpets, I vacuum cleaned, I washed linoleum and the paint on walls and woodwork, I dusted, I did the windows, I polished furniture and wooden floors – and the result was very gratifying, if a little shabby.

I was bringing the place back to life as it had been and it was an extremely gradual process. It was also a process that, in a way, not only started in a real sense with the first action but, once restarted, could be seen as not having terminated and as continuing. I mean the first time I cleaned a particular carpet was only the next time after the last time it had been done, and it was just something that went on being done. I picked up where things had been left off – I did the laundry, washed the dishes, cleared out and relaid the fire, finished the lavatory paper and put another roll in its place.

Things that needed mending I had to take one at a time and depending. There were the light injuries, so to speak – picture frames which were broken or with the glass shattered and even some furniture which only required glueing and cramping. Then there were the more severe casualties, large and small. One I remember was a foot square pasteboard set of filing drawers which had doubtless been quite literally kicked around. It was completely worthless but what I did was to laboriously steam the paper covering off (simulated snake skin!), rebuild the carcase, back the paper, and then reapply it, pinching what had been on the bottom to fill in elsewhere. I also did things which at least look more difficult; I actually found most of what needed to be done simple if reduced to tasks and tackled methodically. Here I suppose I'm talking about the likes of re-laying and patching veneer or actually replacing a missing cupboard door of a pair and getting the build, stain, sheen, and distress just right.

But some repairs were quite beyond me – a case in point being the charred furniture in the mausoleum. Some replacement bits had to be specially turned and the sofa, of course, had to be completely stripped down and rebuilt. This was where – and not only this – I ran into not so much a credibility as an incredulity problem. The people I took the likes of this to told me plainly that the cost of what would need to be done was far beyond the possible worth. I had to plead with them and make all sorts of special cases and excuses – both to rationalize and in order to encourage them to waste their professional time. Like the man who came to convert the ancient grey enamel gas cooker to North Sea Gas; I don't know quite how I got him to do it.

The reactions of such people did, I confess, on occasion make me think momentarily about what I was doing. I knew then that it was odd behaviour – as I know now – but the urge was very strong (I believe I have used the word instinctive) and I certainly have no regrets in retrospect. I couldn't rationally explain it at first and I'm not sure that I can now. But let me say that I was entirely comfortable with the whole operation; it was an enormous pleasure in prospect, a case of joyous involvement in the doing, and completion of any part not only gave great satisfaction but added to the total which I was so felicitously at home within. This was the strange part at the nub of it; it wasn't, to me, that I was restoring a world that belonged to someone else, as a museum curator might – no, I felt that I was reinstating an environment that belonged to me as no other had.

Margaret, of course, was very much a part of all this and I would go up the road to see her quite frequently. Not that frequently, mind, perhaps only once every two weeks, for there always existed a kind of reserve that killed any tendency to intimacy in its tracks. I could never, for example, have taken her out in the car, or given her anything that might be construed as personal – and the idea of her coming to or staying over in the house was a long way down the road of impossibility, regardless of her frailty and the polite fictions about the house that existed. I sort of felt that I had to have a reason for going to see her. The artificiality of the relationship was nowhere more apparent than with regard to the house. I was, after all, going to see her after recreating some small part of what had been, while the fiction she continued (and I supported her in) was that it was still as she had left it. The result was that I didn't tell her what I'd been doing and she didn't ask any questions. Instead – because the house was our principal point of contact – she would talk about it at great length, but on the basis of memory. And as far as it became a conversation – and it did – I relied as much on what I had put together from her reminiscences as I did on my everyday experience.

But what this did mean from the point of view of 'putting things to rights' was that I could work out in large measure what was missing by her descriptions – and, providing I approached it in the right way, it was possible for me to direct any enquiry to particular areas and in the greatest detail. I could find out, for example, where the old newspapers had been stored (and which newspapers) or where the darning mushroom had been kept. And if there were marks on the wall or nails which indicated a missing picture or ornamental weapon then I stood a very good chance of finding out exactly what it had been.

This all encouraged and assisted me in the matter of replacing things that had gone. I travelled around quite extensively (I didn't look in Ramsgate), going round junk yards, antique shops, etc. In point of fact, some of my greatest successes came through writing to trade specialists. By far the most surefire way of acquiring any particular piece of Indian armour or weaponry, strange to say, is to have it sent from America, while prints and paintings are better obtained through a number of London shops. I hope I am not giving the impression here that all the things I replaced were what might be considered collectors' pieces – for that was far from the case. A lot of what I was looking for was pure junk – post-war crockery and the like – though I was to find that valve radios had become collectable.

The perhaps surprising thing is that in reinstating the house I did not end up with something that was static or sterile. Far from it. The 'camping equipment' I had brought with me was out of place and was disposed of as it seemed right, but a lot of things I had brought were of a personal nature in that they had association and meaning and I actually found it easy and harmonious to integrate these. One case in point that went even further than this was putting my own coin collection in the display cabinet that Margaret's first husband had reused, even though I found a listing of what had been there. And I found myself buying things for the house in general, living in it, redecorating here and there, with the sense that I was not destroying anything but continuing it.

I have said that I found the house to be an environment that belonged to me as no other had. It was home, it was me, it made me feel happy and fulfilled, it was a coherent, harmonious expression of my being. Oh dear, that past tense is so ominous and where I am is so ghastly. This cold makes things worse.

XXVII

I did mention the body in the mausoleum and the fact is, it's still there. After I'd taken the furnishings and rubbish out I carefully removed the smoke and graffiti from the walls and ceiling and not merely swept, but vacuumed the floor (and the passages), the whole being lit by argon lights from a trailing flex. I reblocked our original way in – from the sea side – using the same bricks which James and I had taken out, cementing them in place from the outside using mortar. When the piece of internal decorated plaster I'd cut out had been replaced and fudged in then you could see nothing. Given the damaged condition of the bones, the reconstruction of a perfect skeleton was hardly on the cards but I did do my best. With the access from the house, I rebricked it, had someone in to plaster (that's beyond me) and then used matching wallpaper which I peeled from the adjacent entrance hall.

It wasn't perfect but then I didn't think perfection was appropriate. While I couldn't do anything about it I very much regretted that the skeleton was in such a condition, but I was pleased that the grave goods weren't there – there seemed something off about their being put in in the first place. And while I did go some way in that direction I didn't believe the astute would be fooled by my handiwork – any more than I had been by that of my predecessors. I left the filled teeth in the skull. Also, while I made damned sure that no one would find their way from the sea side – by collapsing the tunnel – I felt the situation at the house end could only be as it had been.

But I am worried here, as I am, in these drawn out days with little and so much to think about. Partly it is on the score of the house and the mausoleum being intruded upon again; the latter could cause questions to be asked, which might be awkward, but it's the general violation which I most fear. Anyone who has suffered burglary must know and Margaret must have been in awful anguish, the house being such a personal thing to her, as to me. I solved the problem for her (though only after years) but who is there to do the same for me? No one, I am entirely alone. And it goes further for I realize how desperately I care what happens to that house after my death – and there is nothing I can do about it.

Even admitting mortality, men have hoped that something would survive of them and of others whom they value: possessions, family ties, ideals, ideas, whatever. But it only takes a moment's thought to see that what we might regard as a wealth of heritage in fact underlines how almost total the loss is. Virtually everything that is kept in the memory – imperfectly and partially – is lost two generations beyond a person's life. We live in a crust on the surface of history and whatever we dredge up from below and carry along with us it is but a poor, simplified, generalized, inaccurate, infinitismally small fraction of what has gone. And go back a few generations, and then a few more – well it's obvious. Look at the great Clodius Albinus – what, and with uncertainty, do we know about him? The sum total could be (has been!) written down in a few hundred words, and he was one of the important few, after man had been around for ninety-nine per cent of his time, and in a culture which has survived by adoption. What of his contemporaries; the multitudes then, before and after; what about the rest of the world? He had a name and dates – essential visas you don't get anywhere without, but which you don't necessarily get anywhere with. Frankly, who cares, and who can care? Those who live can only dabble in the past as far as it serves their interests, instructs, or amuses. Those who die delude themselves if they think they leave anything that a tide or two will not efface. Still, it is hard to think of everything going, perhaps harder than thinking of my own end.

This is because, as I have said, I found my self with the house; the irony of its importance to me is that I lived before among external matters; the resolution of what I'm saying, I suppose, is that the house constituted a medium which was an exact fit. But why? It puzzled me, and I felt there had to be a reason.

I realized when I first went in the house – that night when I explored it in the darkness and James was left by the Tilly lamp in the mausoleum – I realized then that I had been there before. This feeling never left me; it's part of why I took on, as natural, the peculiar task of looking after the house, and it was always familiar to me. There was also, of course, the point that my mother knew Margaret and – seemingly uniquely – knew her in connection with the house. And I tackled Margaret head on about it – well, perhaps a little tentatively and when I was a bit more certain in my own mind than I make out I had been. I told her, I said:

'Do you know, I always feel as though I've been in that house. A long time ago.'

'Do you really?' she replied, rather absently.

'You knew my mother, didn't you?' I persisted.

'Well yes, that's right dear, you know that, and the two things go together you see.' She was thinking while she was talking. 'As I remember it, your mother knocked on the door – we didn't get callers – because you'd fallen over on some glass outside and she was panicking and needed a bandage. Do you remember?'

I said that I didn't, but I also said, 'I hardly think that once would account for what I do remember; it's not the detail – which is vague – it's that I feel I know every part of the house.'

'Oh, well, she came back a few times after that dear. Probably first she brought a few cakes or something to thank me for the trouble. She would have brought you. I imagine she used to take you to the West Cliff bandstand – a band in red jackets played there every afternoon in summer. Do you remember? I often used to sit out on the balcony with the second Eddy and listen and I used to see a lot of mothers with their children.'

Margaret was getting uncomfortable, not wanting to talk, sending out signals that it was forbidden territory; still, while backing off, I wanted to hold ground.

'So, my mother became a friend of yours and she and I visited you and the second Eddy when I was small,' I volunteered this, offering it as an end.

Margaret hesitated, wheels turning in her mind. 'Your mother, Jonathan, might have liked to have been a friend and to have popped in and out and all of that, but the more it became so – and it was more her way than mine – the more obvious the impossibility was. The second Eddy and I had to keep ourselves to ourselves and I'm afraid we were forced to put your mother off.'

'Do you remember me,' I asked. 'How old was I?'

Margaret took her glasses off, a bad sign or, at least, a signal of finality. 'I do remember you, but not at all well, and I also remember that you'd just had your fourth birthday when I last saw you.'

This was what I went away with and it was soon after I moved to Ramsgate, in fact shortly before I went to see my father 'from London' for the first time. It sounds interesting, perhaps little enough

– a simple explanation – but I dwelt on it, turning things over, adding one conclusion to another, coming up with an answer which was very central to my being from then on. The big thing I came to – and it was so obvious – was that I was Margaret's child. Everything pointed to it; it made sense. She was pregnant by her second husband when she remet her first; if I wasn't the child then where was it – she'd never said anything. Presumably the second Eddy hadn't wanted me around and I'd been disposed of by a means amounting to adoption. I couldn't be sure about the details of this but perhaps it had happened at the age of four – this would fit with my memories and what Margaret hadn't quite said – or, alternatively, I'd maybe been brought to visit my mother up to that age. Why else would Margaret have summoned me – she seemed to think she had, though puzzled by the delay. Why else, after all, would she have handed everything over in the way she did – lock, stock and barrel? And, you see, she would only have been doing what was right in that respect; she and the second Eddy may have made improper use of my father's estate but it was being restored to his heir.

It might be wondered how I took what could be construed as a bit of a bombshell, but the fact is that I eagerly embraced every stage of its unravelling. I hadn't had a good childhood, I'd never felt I'd belonged in my family or that I was understood and cared about; I didn't feel close to either my mother or father; and I'd always taken this to account for difficulties I had in relating to the world and being comfortable with other people. I could add, relating to and being comfortable with myself. What had come along wasn't altogether nice (if I may use that word) but it did have the ring of truth and truth is half way to understanding, itself a necessity for acceptance. Whatever the barbs, it was clearly the better alternative.

It gave me some roots, and existence which I was at one with. Where, before, I had done things with either uncertainty or the feeling that I should; where, before, I had felt strangely displaced from all that was around me; where, before, I had never felt content or happy (though with little reason for disatisfaction); now I had life as I had never known it.

That body in the mausoleum, that was my father – there was something definite and strong to it. My mother, Margaret, was aged and spending her last years in comfort a walk away. I couldn't know the one and I hardly knew the other; many aspects of what must have happened were deeply upsetting; but it was a saga which had power and energy – and to which I belonged. To start with, my father was in Africa (his uncle in the Colonial Service); my mother had thrown up a 'good' family background for love; there was love, there was intrigue, there was suspicious death. And I was a part of it all.

I went through and through the contents of that house, sifting, sorting, looking for clues. There were some letters, a few documents, my mother's childhood diaries, books with inscriptions in and – best of all – there were photographs, some with names, dates, places. Using the available information I was able to continue the process of putting together who I was. I, of course, used information which I had got from my mother and I went back to her time and time again and, on the pretext of talking about the house, I found out a little bit more about this or that, and I gradually fitted piece to piece. I didn't stop there either for I did a documentary search of my mother's family, my father's family, and my stepfather's family, I found both wedding certificates and – I tell you, this was something – I found what I instinctively knew to be my own true birth certificate: I was John Edward Creswell and, as importantly, there was my proper date of birth, a few days different. I had a name and I had a date! The parallels between what I had done for myself and what I had done for Clodius Albinus were not lost on me – I found it rather amusing.

You may wonder why I wasn't more direct with Margaret who, after all, I had worked out was my mother. But the fact was that I knew – on the basis of what I had experienced of her – that her responses were likely to be negative and reluctant and I did not wish to risk that. I was content to have the knowledge that I had and to play a game with her rather like that we played about the house. With the house we never alluded to it being anything other than it had been, talking about it for hours upon end, but deliberately skirting round any admission of the reality. Similarly, we kept up the fiction about me and, indeed, of her having had a child, but talked in detail – albeit one step at a time – about my family and background.

I could also see it from her side. She'd lived her life under the oppression of great upsets, strains, shocks, tensions and she had come to an accommodation in her old age which she could live with and which she didn't want to leave. I could understand that and I was actually happy for her.

It was in the whole context that I lived in and restored the house. It was my family home, everything in it was my inheritance, I could just relax and be myself. I had a certain amount of money – not much when Margaret was alive – but enough for my restoration and research projects and to keep me from having to earn an income. I sat and I thought rather a lot and I got into the habit of 'being' rather than 'doing'. I read, I pottered around, mused over things I'd collected and – most of all – I reflected quietly and with inner contentment. This was something I'd always been too busy to do, or never had the opportunity, or – more realistically – had never had the capacity for, never valued, never had the necessary inner peace.

While the house and all about me there was what I fitted into, it is interesting that, bit by bit, I began to look outward too. As I have said, I disliked Ramsgate, and I had disliked it for as long as I knew but I found myself going out and looking around, at first – when my father was alive – by late evening and night. What I discovered – or rediscovered – were elements I had fond memories of back over the years and as time went by I explored the hinterland too, reuniting myself, making what I related to back into a part of me.

Even if I could have formerly imagined it – which would have been impossible – I could never have believed that I would ever have become so content and fulfilled. For me it was like finding a new world or heightened plane within an existence of which I had previously had but a blinkered, low and cowed perception.

XXVIII

Small wonder I find this wretched place so difficult. I wish I was back in the house – but I know I'll never see it again. I'd like to die there, not here. You know, I have nothing here except my self and while this is still strong – as it was in the house – I don't like the situation I find myself in. It's like trying to keep your dignity when you've lost your clothes. No, it *was* like that; then there was a phase of going through the motions without thinking too hard about the situation; now, it sometimes seems pointless. Writing what I have written has kept me together in the face of death, estrangement and boredom. It's done a lot more than keep me occupied and it's been much more than a diversion; it's been a small emergency system for keeping my self together.

But I feel so desperately ill – I heard pneumonia mentioned – they've certainly been tapping around and listening – and the fact is that I can't write. I suppose I must have acquired some sort of cachet here as a character; maybe they're going to find out all about me when I'm dead; anyway they supplied me, unbidden, with a little tape recorder. I'm glad, I'll actually play it back and write everything out that I've said when I feel better, and then I'll have to think what to do with what I've written as a whole. What I want to do just now is to finish off what I was saying about Margaret – Margaret and me – I was half way through that. I do feel self-conscious though, muttering into my pillow; I must have attracted attention before – my goodness, they've all changed, I can't remember them – but, scribbling, I didn't notice.

When Margaret died, I took it very easily. I may have said all this before, I don't know. Her position was, of course, in several ways like mine is – estranged, lonely, fearful, awaiting death – but I admired her equanimity. Mind, I only saw from the outside, and what does one see from the outside? – what does this lot here make of me, I wonder? But she seemed very much to have come to terms with everything; I felt that she'd thought her own way through in long hours. I suppose she had a better start than me and three decades more to do it in. I wish we'd talked, even given what I know – me as me, and her as her – but we didn't have that sort of relationship and, in any case, who would have known I would be dying so soon after? Her death, though, seemed right and natural and no cause for distress and that's important, if only as an example.

It was my mother that I buried. I chose the scantest ceremony – she had no religious beliefs that I knew of – and only the solicitor, a representative of the home, and I were there. It seemed right to make as little of the event as possible. I intended to put half of her ashes with each of her husbands but, by dint of never doing it, I kept them. They'll still be there, in the house.

I said it was my mother I buried – if putting cremated remains on a shelf is burying – but I had yet to collect her few belongings from the home. There among them was a picture of the baby I knew in a frame and, behind it and folded together, were the birth certificate of John Edward Creswell – which I had seen the copy of – and, also, the certificate of his death at the age of four. I wasn't him; he hadn't been me; Margaret wasn't my mother; the whole background I'd put together for myself was nonsense; and I was as I had been.

But was I? It was a blow – I won't pretend it wasn't – and it took me a long time to come out of the shock. I had borrowed clothing for myself, that was true, clothing which – it turned out – did not belong to me. But it also turned out that it was more me than what I had had and by finding my environment *I*, if you like, was more than I had ever been. There was no going back, I belonged – I still belong – to where I am; it is the past that I came out of that is foreign.

And I am not speaking here of differences in wealth, of material possessions, of standards of living, for in ways I have actually become poorer (or at least unambitious) in these respects. Nor am I talking about achievement for I had – singularly – 'got on' to outward appearance, and I have relinquished all that to be a nothing in such terms. Contentment and a sense of position and worth are what I have; they are assets which I would have formerly been as unable to recognize, value or defend, as I now find it unnecessary to do anything overt about them. It's all as it is, it's my life and I don't have to construct it, tend it, or answer questions.

Why wasn't I happy being as I was born? Maybe there's a large answer here which goes to the root of why human society has evolved as dynamically as it has – but that would be explaining an individual's hunger in terms of Malthus or a person's looks in terms of Darwin. What concoction of circumstance and innate faculties was it for me? I could pick over the past – remembered, half remembered, supposed and invented – but, aside from my cautionary experience as John Edward Creswell, I feel (now) that the causes do not matter. I also feel now that one has to accept the pain and the hurt of such circumstance as just being a part of existence, as with childbirth, illness, injury, death. It's fine me saying that now – it doesn't help me as I was so long ago, young, bewildered, distressed – but I have come to terms with the experience. I don't have to feel guilty, or explain, or evaluate; it was as it was.

It was not coming to terms with it, I suppose, that kept me in that dreadful no-man's-land, that limbo of unbelonging, for so long. It was that existence of little-ease that I had sought to save James from, realizing that I'd taken him so far and then shaking him off in the hope that he would go back. He never suffered the problem, for a different reason, but I couldn't know whether he would alternatively have spent a life thinking what might have been. (Mind, well handled, that can be a limitless luxury.) But what I didn't understand was that the key to release wasn't knowing the destination, it wasn't the effort put into the struggle, and it wasn't the achievement of the aim of acceptance by others. No, important as all of these may be, there can be no release until the past is settled. And then it's like cock-crow scattering the spectres; difficult to know what the problem was.

This is the final chapter and, somehow, I know it. If it's not the end of me – which it may well be – I feel it is probably the end of my quest. No, not quest, that's the wrong word, it implies some grail, some solution that has to be sought and found. What I speak of comes out of a disharmony, a discordance, its very corruption the driving power which – if harnessed and well directed – leads on to its own dissolution, turns back the canker and quenches the fires within. And it is within, that is where the resolution is, not on the vast canvas of eternal truth and reason.

I used the analogy before – or, at least, I think I did – of peeling back the layers of an onion. I felt that I had lived on the surface of things, conscious of pain within but with no understanding of it. Going into the layer below would increase the discomfort but lead me closer to the truth. And I am sure that I thought that by repeating this process, layer by layer, I would progressively near the centre of things. I now realize the analogy – as with most taken for something not understood – is imperfect. In a small way it shows how poorly reality fits our models and the futility of mapping the inaccessible and devoutly believing; it has no impact on the truth. But I give this too much weight. The fact is – and to put things simply – I have looked behind the superficial, to great effect, and having achieved this end I have no impulse to go further, I don't know whether further exists, and I don't care. If the analogy was a possession then, albeit once valued, it would now be somewhere in the back of a drawer. Perhaps there could be a trunk in the attic too, a big one, for all the conjectures there have been about man within greater existence.

'So, is being at one with oneself as far as can be gone?'

'I suppose there are things that enhance – like being able to appreciate value, the pursuit of truth, adding rather than taking away – but yes.'

'Value and truth change, don't they? You know that and "adding to" assumes direction and improvement. Well . . .?'

'Perhaps then it's relative to one's own time and condition.'

'Ephemeral, relative, inconstant – the certainties of one era are illusions seen from another. Do you mean that illusion is sufficient?'

'I suppose so, though I'm reluctant to admit that delusion is desirable.'

'Even if its effect is the same.'

'Yes. Because it warps at any one time how life can be viewed and life is the certainty.'

'So there's life as well as being at one with oneself? Should the one be spent in pursuit of the other?'

'From preference no, but it's little use without it.'

'Have not some of the greatest contributors been the most distressed as individuals?'

'That is true.'

'And, so, does it matter – depending on the viewpoint – does contentment matter that much?'

'I don't suppose it does really, it is nothing in the scale of things.'

'Even having existed?'

'No.'

'Would it have mattered if you'd actually been John Creswell?'

'No, nor if I'd been Clodius Albinus.'

'Or the person whose bones you took for his?'

'Or the Roman whose grave it really had been.'

'Or any person, or any construction of them, even if it was untrue?'

'Well, it wouldn't have mattered.'

'Nothing seems to have mattered and it is such a minimal view you have. What happened to the vital importance of who you were, of time and place, of the core of meaning, of the meaning of existence, of the existence of endless stimulation in scale and scope?'

'I know what you mean and I can't be bothered. Even thinking about it is too much. I'm ill you know.'

'You're ill. Are you dying? Does this have to do with it?'

'I suppose so, I suppose that all the concerns and interests you speak of are those of the living. They are essentially a part of life; perhaps they only exist in life. It's like trying to recapture what was so very important when a particular age; one can only catch the ghost of it.'

'Would you want to go back?'

'Oh no, I really couldn't be bothered.'

'Is this the end then?'

'Yes.'

'There is nothing else?'

'No.'

'Are you sure? Content? Sure you're sure? Very well.'